Hold On
to Love

Also by
MOLLIE HUNTER

The Knight of the Golden Plain
You Never Knew Her as I Did
The Third Eye
A Furl of Fairy Wind
The Wicked One
The Kelpie's Pearls
A Stranger Came Ashore
The Stronghold
The Haunted Mountain
A Sound of Chariots
The Thirteenth Member
The Walking Stones

Talent Is Not Enough:
Mollie Hunter on Writing for Children

Mollie Hunter

Hold On to Love

1 8 🔥 1 7

———— HARPER & ROW, PUBLISHERS ————

Cambridge, Philadelphia, San Francisco, London, Mexico City, São Paulo, Sydney

———— NEW YORK ————

✳

To Norah, with love
            M.H.

Part One

I

The pain hit Bridie in mid stride. She dealt with it as she had before, holding hard with her left hand to the iron railings that lined the pavement, slackening tension on the area of pain by raising her right foot from the ground. Half doubled over, she judged the approach of the second when the whole of her right side would be flaring with pain; then, with the hard edges of her night-school books jammed against the soft flesh beneath her chin, she created the distraction of a different kind of pain. She counted. Last time she had reached twenty-five before the force of the attack had died away into the kind of ache she had learned to accept as bearable.

    —twenty-nine, thirty. Was it safe now to stand straight?
Cautiously she let her right foot settle back onto

the pavement and allowed her grip on the railings to loosen. It would be all right, she reckoned. She wouldn't be able to run down the rest of the street, and that meant she'd be late for night school. But it would still be all right for her to walk. With her books held well away from contact with the tender area that was the outward sign of the ache in her lower right side, she began walking towards the distant mark of the school's lit bell tower.

Just ahead on the opposite side of the street there were other lights. Bellwood Hall—there was always a dance on there Friday nights: people waltzing, fox-trotting, sitting with their arms around one another's shoulders, talking, laughing . . . How did you get yourself invited to a dance? There was no one on the dark street except herself, books under her arm, head turned for a quick glance towards the shift of figures and smiling faces behind the unscreened windows of Bell-wood Hall.

Music spilled onto the street as she passed, and she wondered how many other parties like this one were going on that night in Edinburgh. Envy rose higher in her, so that walking through the sound of the music felt like wading through a tide that threatened to become deep enough to choke the breath from her.

She began to hurry again, protecting herself against the fear of the pain returning by thinking that to-morrow she really would have to speak to Granny about it. Or maybe she would write home and let Mum know how bad it could be. The smell of the school corridors engulfed her—chalk, sweat, dust—Bellwood High was such a crummy place! Dark wood and frosted glass of the door that carried the dog-eared card announcing MR. KENDALL. ADVANCED ENGLISH. Then she was sliding into her seat, blushing as usual at the grin the dark-haired boy, Peter McKinley, always flashed at her, yet still as usual ignoring the grin and staring down instead at the scuffed blue cover of last week's corrected work.

"I'll mark you present—but only just," Mr. Kendall said drily.

She nodded and told him, "I brought that—you know, that stuff I said I would."

Carefully she slid to one side of her desk the big, battered envelope that contained her poems. Kendall glanced briefly towards it, and then focused on the class to say briskly, "One foolscap page now from each of you on the function of the apostrophe. *With* examples. And remember that handwriting will count—especially for those of you who hope to sit for the Civil Service exams."

Bridie bent her head along with the rest of the class. All around her the rustle of paper and the muttering of exchanged remarks gave way to a silence of concentration that remained unbroken till there was the sound of a smothered laugh from far back in the classroom. Kendall said quietly,

"Night school, McKinley, is for those who are prepared to work at a subject. There is no need to be in my class if you do not fall into that category."

To show the use of the apostrophe, one could say, "Peter McKinley's dark, Peter McKinley's handsome. . . ."

5

In hasty embarrassment at herself, Bridie pushed aside her wandering thought and the impulse to write it on the paper before her. Mr. Kendall's hand appeared on the envelope at the side of her desk. Smoothly he slid it into his grasp before he continued his walk up the aisle between the rows of desks, and too late then she recalled what he had told her last week when he had asked to see some of her poems.

"But don't be obvious about handing them over, Bridie. End of the session, say—that might be the best time. I can't have the rest of your class think I'm playing favorites."

He'd be angry with her now, she thought, for mentioning the damned things the moment she'd come in—maybe wouldn't like them, because of that. Then he wouldn't speak to his editor friend about them, and she didn't know anybody except him who had an editor friend, and so she'd never get them published. The pain attacked her again, like an enemy suddenly stabbing her in the side, and this time there was no counting, no struggle. This time, the pain had won. The scream it drew from her began as she slid sideways along her desk, and was sounding still as she toppled to the wooden floor of the classroom.

2

She was in a small room with walls and ceiling of dazzling white. There was a blanket over her. She was lying on something that had a rigid surface, but there was a muzziness in her brain that made her feel she was floating. Voices sounded through the muzziness, getting louder, fading again. . . .

A man's voice first. "What's her family situation?"

A woman's voice. "The father's dead. We couldn't have risked waiting for the mother to get here, either, because she lives too far out of town."

The man. "And so what *did* you do about the consent form?"

The woman. "Oh, you don't have to worry about that. The girl herself has a job that means her home's in town with grandparents and an uncle. We got a police call out to them."

The man. "That must have given them a scare!"

The woman. "M-hmmm. The uncle was in a bit of a state when he arrived here. But he signed the consent without any bother."

"Well, so far so good. And that jab should hold her till we can get her into theater."

"Are you sure, doctor? She struck me as a resistant type."

"Oh, she might come round for a moment or two. But she'll slide off again."

"I hope you're right. With an appendix like she's got—"

"Yes, it's pretty nasty. Don't know when I've ever seen such a rigid abdomen, in fact."

Memory began to come back to Bridie. She was lying on a trolley. Before that there had been an ambulance. And before that again, the floor coming up to meet her, and out of the confusion then the sound of Peter McKinley's voice desperately assuring her, *"It's all right, it's all right, I'll get an ambulance."* After the ambulance ride there had been the feeling of being carried into the hospital under a night sky that seemed enormously remote and swirling with millions of stars. It had given her a terrible sense of aloneness to look up at those stars!

They had done gruesome things to her after that— an enema, shaving her body hair. There had been a doctor—that was him behind her now. She could recognize his voice. And a Sister. The woman behind her was the pleasant, red-faced Sister MacPherson who had said, "No, no, Bridie, you're far too young to sign the consent form yourself. You're only fifteen and a half!" Then the doctor had given her a jab of something that had made her feel sleepy, so sleepy. . . .

Bridie tried to fight against the slide back into unconsciousness, annoyed at her own seeming weakness, resenting the fact that she had allowed the doctor to give her the injection in the first place. She was a poet, wasn't she? She ought to have stayed alert so that she could use this experience—make *something* of it in words. Those dreadful moments of feeling so alone and helpless under the great swirl of uncaring stars; there was a poem in that, surely? And she ought to be thinking of it now. Stars, stars, what could she find to rhyme with stars . . .

The trolley moved. Rubber wheels whirred faintly somewhere beneath her—far beneath her, it seemed— as the trolley bore her below a long strip of ceiling and into some other place, a white and shadowless place fiercely lit by an overhead light that was like an imprisoned sun glaring down on her.

There were figures moving about in the sun's white prison, white-robed, white-masked figures. One of them, she reasoned dully, must be the prison's Chief Jailer, because everybody addressed him very respectfully as "sir." Hands bore her up from the trolley and laid her on a hard surface directly below the big light. Sir came and leaned over her, looking down into her face. She could see nothing of his face except eyes, and thin black eyebrows. The eyes were brown, and bright, and kind-looking. She wondered about a man in his position having such kind eyes and wanted to speak about them, but could manage only a drowsy question.

"*Are* you the Chief Jailer?"

The brown eyes grew brighter yet with laughter. There was laughter too in the muffled answer from behind the mask.

"I'm your surgeon, Mr. Wright."

His voice sounded very English. Between this and her drowsiness it was hard to make out what he was saying.

"And don't worry, my dear." The kind, bright eyes were still smiling down at her. The blurred impact of his foreign-sounding voice was still reaching her. "All my experience as a surgeon here has taught me that you Scots are a hardy race, and the young ones are the toughest of the lot. Just breathe deeply now, and I'll have you right as rain again in no time at all."

From somewhere behind his right shoulder then, a hand appeared guiding a big, black-rimmed metal nozzle. Bridie had time to realize she was seeing an anesthesia mask; time, before it descended on her, to kick out against the thought of becoming unconscious. Then the rim of the nozzle was pushed against her face, a hard rim that stank of rubber. She was being forced to breathe in a smell other than the rubber—a sweet, sickish smell that was seeping into her brain, destroying Bridie, turning the Bridie who lived centrally in her brain into a whirl of light. . . .

A voice from the pinpoint of black at the core of the light's golden whirl said faintly:

10

"She's fighting it still. Turn that tap further on." . . . *and the light was fragmenting, exploding into millions of stars spinning in an immense dark-blue vortex, and if she was sucked into the vortex she would be exploded too, fragmented into tiny bits of star, she would die, and if only she had believed in God, and the stars were all coming together and forming letters, great shining capital letters that said GOD and there was nothing but that word and it was bearing down on her roaring; the word had a voice and it was roaring at her and she had died. . . .*

3

Bridie surfaced slowly from the drugged sleep that had followed her first return to consciousness. It was morning, and she was in a bed in a ward of the hospital. She felt sick. There was a throb of pain from the wound the surgeon had made. A nurse came to lean over her and say,

"Listen, hen. There's somebody called Peter Mc-Kinley—the young chap that called the ambulance for you—keeps phoning to ask about you. But we're not allowed to give out information except to relatives—unless, maybe, there's something *you* want to tell him?"

"Not really," Bridie managed in a voice that surprised her by its weakness. "Just that I'm all right, I suppose. And of course—er"—she fumbled the words,

afraid the nurse would laugh at them—"that I'm—
er—very grateful to him. For calling the ambulance,
that is."

The nurse didn't laugh. Bridie watched her disappearing form and became aware that she, in turn, was
being watched. On the other side of the ward there
was a large, fat woman sitting up in a bed next to one
occupied by a thin woman with straggly ginger hair.
In a tone that somehow succeeded in mixing sympathy with ghoulish interest, the fat woman asked,

"Was it your womb, hen?"

"Appendix." It was all Bridie felt inclined to say
then; which was probably just as well, she thought,
since even this brief answer was almost lost in the
sound of the ginger-haired woman snorting,

"Don't be daft, Liz. When did one as young as her
have bother wi' her womb!"

"My sister's lassie," Liz began, "when she was only
fourteen, *I'm* telling *you*, Chrissie Telfer, she had to
have this operation for her periods—"

Bridie closed her eyes and lay thinking with wonder
of Peter McKinley phoning the hospital. And phoning,
and phoning again . . . The thought was carried away
in a wave of sleep that was restful this time, with no
nightmare aftermath of the operation in it. When she
woke again it was afternoon. The ward had filled up
with visitors, and her mother was sitting beside the
bed with her young brother, William, standing at the
foot of it.

William looked scared. His eyes were big in his thin,
almost-twelve-year-old's face, and his short fair hair

13

stood up in spikes the way it always did when anxiety made him run his hands through it. She smiled at him, loving him anew for his concern, and to reassure him she teased him about the rumpled hair.

"You're all spiky again," she said. "Like a young hedgehog!"

William smiled with relief at her joke, but she herself was alarmed to realize the continuing feebleness of her voice. With tears beginning to threaten, she turned her head toward her mother and yielded gratefully to the luxury of being cradled in the arm that came reaching out to her.

"There, there, it's all over now." Her mother's voice was calm as always. Her mother's face hovered over her, pink and smooth as rose petals. Her mother, as she had been for more than six years past, was dressed in black. The scent of lavender that hung about her came from the small, lavender-colored scarf that was all she ever permitted to relieve the somber effect of her dress.

"If she were to die," Bridie thought, "this is how I'd always remember her: gentle, always in black, but always pink-cheeked like a rose, and always with the scent of lavender about her."

Her mother was talking, saying that an appendix never failed to give warnings of pain before it got bad enough to need an operation. "And so why didn't you tell us?" she asked. "Why didn't you confide in your granny about the pain? Or tell me about it when you came back to the village for holidays or weekends?"

"My English class," Bridie mumbled into the protecting arm. "You'd have stopped me going out at night to my English class."

"Oh, for goodness' sake! The world wouldn't come to an end if you didn't have lessons in English!"

"It would for me!" Swiftly, on the words, Bridie drew back from her mother. "I've told you before, Mum, writing poetry's all that matters to me. But it's hard to do. You have to learn all sorts of things about language before you're good at it. And how could I manage that without my English classes?"

"It's hard to make a living too, Bridie. Especially these days with so many out of work. And you'll have to learn to put your health and strength first if you're to succeed in holding on to your job."

"I'll be all right." Bridie sat up straighter in bed, and looked her mother determinedly in the eye.

William said suddenly,

"Ach, let her alone, Mum. If she's so ready for a fight again, she *will* soon be all right."

Their mother laughed at this. "You should talk!" she retorted. "There's not a pin to choose between you when it comes to being strong willed."

William ignored this, drawing closer to Bridie to say, "Tell us about the operation then. Were you scared?"

She opened her mouth to say how terrified she had been, and was immediately stopped by the protective instinct she had always felt for William. With an inner voice warning, "What if *he* had to go through an operation one day?" she asked instead, "Me scared? Why should I be? There's nothing to an op, you ninny."

15

"You had *us* scared," her mother told her; "last night, when your Uncle George came rushing out to the village to tell us you'd been taken in here. But it wasn't so bad, of course, once I'd phoned and been told you'd come safely through the operation."

"Then I managed to get a whole day off school to visit you," William chimed in; "and so that wasn't so bad either!"

Bridie began to laugh at this and discovered immediately how painful it was to laugh with stitches in. "I should have warned you about that," her mother exclaimed. "Lie still, dearie, and leave the laughing to us. *And* the talking."

Bridie sank back onto her pillows, the renewed sense of her own weakness making her quite content to accept this arrangement; but it seemed no time at all after that when the shrill ringing of a bell somewhere outside the ward announced the end of the half-hour's visiting time. The nurses were already wheeling in trollies for tea by then. The ward was suddenly in commotion with departing visitors all mixed up with the tea trollies, and Bridie barely had time to wave good-bye to her mother and William before she found a cup of tea pushed into her hands and she was once more conscious of the two women across the ward, Fat Liz and the ginger-haired Chrissie Telfer, still in animated conversation with one another.

They were talking about wombs again, a subject that seemed to hold a great fascination for Liz—that, and something she referred to as "it." Bridie sipped at her tea, nibbled the biscuits that had been given her along with it, and tried to figure out what "it" was. But not until the discussion took in Liz's husband John, and something she referred to as his "rights," did light at last dawn. The woman, Bridie realized, was talking about her periods and her fear of having another baby!

"Imagine, Chris," Liz invited, "I'm fifty-one years old, and 'it' has never left me. Fifty-one! And though John's been a good man to me and I'd be the last to deny him his rights, I'm telling you, at my age I just could not manage another baby."

" 'It' left me when I was forty-three," Chris said complacently. "But you could ask Dr. Johnson what to do. I mean, her being a lady doctor, you could speak to her easier than you could to one of them men."

Bridie had a sudden flash of recollection—herself studying a book she had come across accidentally at the foot of a drawer; furtively studying it, because it was all about how *not* to have babies, and her mother would not have tucked it so deep in the drawer unless it was meant to be kept secret. She looked across the ward, wondering why Fat Liz had never thought of getting that kind of book. Fat Liz was saying,

"I will ask her, Chris. This very day I'll say straight out to her, 'Another baby at my time of life, doctor? It would *kill* me!' "

Fat Liz should have been on the stage, Bridie thought. Everything she said was uttered with such an air of drama! *On the stage . . .* She put down her teacup with her mind echoing the thought. Could *she* compose a play around Fat Liz? She had never tried her hand at a play before, and her side wasn't hurting all that much now—not if she was careful to keep still. And not to laugh, of course, the way she had laughed at William. William and Mum—it had been so good to see them again! William and Mum . . .

With post-operation tiredness once more insidiously taking over her mind, Bridie drifted back into sleep. When she woke again, it was to an air of flurry in the ward and the sight of screens being drawn around Fat Liz's bed. There was a woman in white just disappearing out of sight behind the screens. Ginger-haired Chris caught Bridie's eye, then nodded to the screen and mouthed, "Dr. Johnson."

Bridie pulled herself up on her pillows. Chris was also sitting up straight, and so were the various other women in the ward. Bridie felt herself growing as tense as they seemed to be, the drama of her own emergency operation becoming a thing of the past for her in face of this new excitement.

Dr. Johnson reappeared. She was a fair-haired woman, plain of feature, and the look on her face now was one of some bafflement. The nurse on duty at that end of the ward rolled away the screens from Fat Liz's bed, then went back to her office.

"What'd she say? What'd the doctor tell you, Liz?"

With the flick of the nurse's apron disappearing around the door of the office, a barrage of questions broke on Liz, Bridie's voice sounding as loudly as any of the others. But Fat Liz, she realized, was a performer! The spotlight was on her, and she was going to make the most of it. There was much smoothing of covers, a great show of settling herself comfortably on pillows before she began at last,

"Well, I told Dr. Johnson just like I said I would. But I didn't forget to tell her first, mind you, that I have a good man in John, and about him being entitled to his rights. I was fair. I was honest. And she appreciated that because she's a married wife herself, after all, and so she knows what men are like. But—"

Liz paused at this point to look around the ward and ask, "You know that operation I had when they had to cut me open to get at my womb?"

There was a general and impatient murmur of assent, but still Fat Liz was not to be hurried. "Well," she went on, "it seems I missed my chance there because—Dr. Johnson told me—this business of having bairns is all to do with things they call Fallopian tubes. I *think* that's what she called them, anyway; but it was 'tubes,' I'm sure o' that. *And*, it seems, they could have got at those tubes when they had me opened up."

Bridie began to feel a faint nausea. This was all getting too gory, too much a reminder of the bloody cut lying underneath her own dressings. But Fat Liz was still in full spate, telling them all how she had really poured out her heart to Dr. Johnson about having eight bairns already and being feared of having another one at the age of fifty-one.

"And then"—Fat Liz sat forward from her pillows, both arms stretched out in the gesture of making an embrace—"and then Dr. Johnson put her arms round

19

my neck, and she said to me, she said, 'Oh, my dear' "—
Fat Liz tried out the words again, and got even more
emphasis into them the second time—" 'oh, my *dear*!
If I had but known, I would have *cut the tubes!* ' "

It was hopeless trying not to laugh then, Bridie
found. She slid down in her bed, pulling the covers
up over her head, trying to control both her silent
laughter and the pain it brought her. One eye peering
out over the covers told her she was the only one to
be so affected by Liz's story. Everyone else was serious, all of them still solemnly enjoying the drama she
had created for them. Something clicked into place
in Bridie's mind, the way it always did when—from
no more than being aware of something—she suddenly realized the significance of what she was seeing.

These women led *dull* lives. Being in hospital was
maybe the most exciting thing that had ever happened to them. And Fat Liz, with her unintentionally
comic drama, was probably the most exciting person
they had ever met. They *needed* her—or someone like
her. And that was sad, and—and touching, somehow;
the kind of thing that only a poem could capture. Or
was she wrong there? Maybe some other form of writing would be the best way of capturing that funny/
touching atmosphere. A short story, perhaps? Or what
about that play she had thought of earlier. . . .

"Bridie. Bridie McShane."

Bridie came back to the present with a start to find
the Day Sister at the foot of her bed, with Peter
McKinley standing beside her. He was smiling, and
in the pleased surprise of the moment, Bridie found

herself smiling too. The Sister glanced from one to the other, and said primly,

"Now remember, Bridie, your visitor is not a relative, nor is this an official visiting time. And so we're bending the rules a great deal by letting him in. But not for long. And only because he was so helpful in your case. Is that clear?"

"Yes, Sister."

The Sister whisked away in a flutter of white, her back poker straight. With his smile broadening to a grin, Peter asked, "Are they all like that—sergeant-major types?"

"It's just an appearance they put on, I think," Bridie told him. "They're all really very kind. And the rules about visitors *are* strict. My mother was in earlier today, and she told me about them."

Peter had moved to the side of her bed as she spoke. He had a bunch of rather tired-looking Michaelmas daisies in one hand, a wide-brimmed homburg hat in the other. With a glance at the flowers as he laid them on the locker beside the bed, he said apologetically,

"From my mum's garden. They're not much, I'm afraid, but I didn't have time to go into town to buy some decent ones."

It was on the tip of Bridie's tongue to say, "It's the first time anyone's brought me flowers, and I think they're beautiful!" But shyness made her swallow the words. After all, as it had suddenly occurred to her, she and Peter McKinley weren't even friends—just two people who happened to share a class; and they had hardly exchanged more than a sentence before that moment. Besides, he was two and a half years older than herself. She was only a kid to him, and so he was obviously just being kind to her.

"Thank you," she told him instead; and although her voice sounded distant, even to herself, she could not help it. "It was good of you to bother."

"It wasn't any bother." Now he sounded shy. There was an awkward silence that Bridie tried to cover by motioning him to sit on the edge of her bed. As he lowered himself towards it, she said hesitantly,

"They—um—they told me about you phoning."

"Yes." He looked down at his fingers busily smoothing the brim of his hat. "I— Well, you were in such a state when they carted you off, and I—" His eyes met hers again. "I felt sort of responsible for you."

"Because it was you who called the ambulance?"

He laughed a little at this. "Somebody had to do it. You won't remember, I suppose, but Mr. Kendall panicked when you screamed and hit the floor, and so everybody else panicked too."

"Except you."

"I've had some Red Cross training in first aid," he explained. "It doesn't make you skilled, of course, but it does teach you that keeping your head and thinking calmly is the most important thing in an emergency."

"I'm very grateful to you." The shyness in Bridie's voice as she said this seemed to make him shy again also. There was another silence; and again she tried to cover it, chattering this time about how glad she had been of her mother and William's visit because

22

she didn't see them very often now that she had to live with her grandparents.

"It's the cost of the fares home, you see," she explained. "My mother lives quite a way out of town, and my job doesn't pay enough to let me travel back and forth every day. But I'll be spending my convalescence with my mother, thank goodness, and I'm looking forward to that."

"Already?" Peter sounded surprised, as if he had concluded she was under the impression that she could leap out of bed there and then. "I was going to ask how you're feeling," he went on. "But if you're looking that far ahead, I suppose the answer must be that you're feeling all right."

"I am," she assured him. "My wound hurts a bit, of course; but apart from that I really am feeling fine."

"You don't look it." He was staring at her now. He had blue eyes, very blue; and there was something in their stare that made her uncomfortable. He spoke suddenly. "You look very small."

"But I *am* small." Puzzled and protesting, she stared back at him. "I'm not much bigger than my kid brother, and he's hardly twelve yet."

"I didn't mean that," Peter told her. "I meant that you look small just now, the way that even quite sturdy kids do when they're sick in bed with all the bounce gone out of them. 'Fragile' is maybe the word. And small*er*."

"I'll bounce back." Bridie spoke determinedly, pushing away the temptation to luxuriate in this unexpected vision of herself as some little-girl-lost sort of creature. "I'll be all the better, in fact, for losing that crummy appendix; and I'll be back at my job in no time. You'll see!"

Peter had begun to grin at the determined tone. "I'm beginning to see already," he told her. "And I'm also beginning to wonder what sort of a job could possibly need all the energy you usually have."

Bridie hesitated, her glance unwillingly turning to the small, wilted bunch of flowers on her locker. Peter's glance followed her own. As if he had begun to divine what was in her mind, he exclaimed, "Oh, no! Oh, *no!*"

"Oh, yes," she said apologetically. "I'm afraid it's true. I work in a flower shop."

He began to laugh then, a low, amused chuckle she would willingly have joined in, if only her stitches had allowed. She tried, in fact, and then found she had to beg,

"Don't, please. My stitches . . ."

"Yes, Mr. McKinley, the patient's stitches!" The Day Sister had suddenly appeared again, like some guardian Cerberus at the foot of the bed. "We cannot permit either laughter or coughing after an operation. That is the rule. And anyway—" One large and well-scrubbed hand plucked a watch from the top pocket of her apron, and held it out for him to see. "I told you ten minutes, and now your time is up."

Peter got to his feet, face sober again, although the laughter was still in his eyes. "Thank you, Sister, I was just going. And if you could tell me what the official visiting hours are . . . ?"

"Three o'clock to four, Saturdays and Sundays. Three to half past three on Wednesdays, and no more than two visitors per patient at any one time." Mechanically the Sister recited the rules; and smiling again at Bridie, Peter said,

"I'll come again this Saturday or Sunday, then. If I may?"

"But you can't!" Dismayed, Bridie looked from him to the Sister. "My mother, my brother, my uncle, my grandparents—they're all taking turns to come at the weekend. My mother told me so. You wouldn't be allowed, if there's to be no more than two at a time."

"And I can't come next Wednesday afternoon," Peter said, disappointedly, "because I'll be working then."

The Sister drew herself even straighter to announce, "Well, that settles that. Bridie will be out of hospital by the following weekend, and so there's no further need to discuss visiting." With a look that clearly indicated she would brook no further delay, she returned her watch to its pocket; and in a rush of words, Bridie offered:

"But I'll be back at the Bellwood class after my convalescence. Four weeks after they let me out of here."

"I'll look for you there," Peter told her. He smiled, raised a hand in farewell, then followed the Sister's determined exit from the ward, walking as straight as she did and not looking back—although Bridie had the feeling that he wanted to do so.

4

Bridie marked off the last day of her stay in hospital in her pocket diary, then reached into her locker for the pile of paper and pencils her mother had brought her. The play centered on a Fat Liz type of character was proving harder to write than she had supposed, she admitted to herself. It needed a subplot of some kind—but what on earth was the technique of working in a subplot? She looked across the ward, saw that Fat Liz was about to make a pilgrimage to the bathroom, and began critically trying to assess the effect of the woman's appearance.

Liz, she had already realized, was a big woman, bigger even than could be guessed at from any sight of her in bed. Her hair was black and long, and hanging down her back. Her features were in keeping with her frame: big, bold features, only slightly blurred by the fattiness of her flesh. The robe she wore now was a long one, Imperial purple in color; and dressed in it, with the slow and stately movements that were her usual mode of progress, she looked like a Queen. A Queen . . .

Still looking at Fat Liz, Bridie groped blindly for her pencil. The Queen, as their eyes met, winked at her, and cheerfully asked,

"You're about ready for the off, then?"

"Couldn't be readier," Bridie agreed; and on the impulse then, it seemed, Fat Liz veered off her course towards the bathroom. The big body plumped itself down on Bridie's bed, the big bold face leaned, smiling, towards Bridie herself; and with the air of one about to embark on confidence in return for confidence, Liz told her,

"Aye, but you're one o' the lucky ones! You've got a job to go to. And my man, my John, says this unemployment will get worse before it gets better. Two years now he's been on the dole—1935 was the last time he brought home a wage. And that's bad for a man's pride."

"So how do you manage?" The woman was working around to something, Bridie realized, but still she could not resist being drawn along the way Fat Liz seemed to want her to go. "How d'you manage to feed all those kids of yours, Liz?"

"I clean floors," Liz said. "I scrub my hands raw, hen. And that's no pleasure, I can tell you."

"The Matron offered me a job like that," Bridie

27

confessed. "One day when she was on her rounds. Said a strong young girl like me would be fit again in no time. But she didn't know, of course, that I had a job to go back to, and she was doing me a favor by her way of it."

"Some favor!" Fat Liz laughed, her usual rich, chortling laugh. "You'd have been worked to a shadow under *that* snooty old biddy. But . . . eh . . ." She paused, and Bridie guessed she was about to hear the real reason for the conversation. ". . . tell me now, hen, what sort of job is it you have?"

"I work in a flower shop. All my mum's folk are in that trade, and I'm apprenticed to it."

"With them?"

Bridie nodded. "My grandpa's in the wholesale line. But he has shops as well. He and my Uncle George are Thomas Armstrong & Son."

Fat Liz looked impressed. "You must be well off!"

Bridie said emphatically, "Don't you believe it! My mum married a man without a penny to his name. Then she was widowed, and so we've always been the poor end of the family."

"But her folks—"

"Never gave her anything but sympathy," Bridie interrupted. "And as for me, I get my keep and an apprentice wage that doesn't do much more than pay my night school fees."

"So, you're studyin', are you?" Liz's eyes gleamed at this further bit of information. "I thought that, the way you're forever write, write, writin' away there. But what're you studyin' *for*, hen?"

"To be a writer," Bridie said; and the sense of elation she felt in saying the words so confidently brought a broad smile to her face. "To be a better writer than I already am, I mean. And I'll tell you something else, Liz. All that writing you've seen me do means I'm working on something at this very moment!"

"Well, I declare!" Liz straightened up, making a great show of amazement, but still not quite managing to hide the suspicion that had leapt suddenly into her eyes. "And what would that be about, hen? Some o' the nurses here, maybe? Or even . . ." Her gaze narrowed, became even more suspicious. "Or even just ordinary folk—like me, for instance?"

"Och, Liz!" Bridie leaned back on her pillows, laughing. "You don't have to be afraid of me or anyone else writing about you, because you're *not* ordinary. You're great! A once-off, in fact. And anybody that does write about you would be bound to make you into something magnificent, like a— Well, I'll be honest and tell you what I'd do with you. I'd make you a Queen!"

Fat Liz laughed her rich laugh. "You'd have a job on your hands—me, a cleaning woman." Stately in her purple robe, she rose and stood looking down at Bridie. "As for you bein' a writer," she said genially, "that might be true and it might no'. But you're still a right daft wee gomeril, because the only kind o' Queen *I'll* ever be is Queen o' Hearts to my bairns and to my man, my John!"

Chuckling still, she took up her interrupted pilgrimage. Bridie lay savoring the memory of their conversation, and wondering how she could fit it into the train of thought that had started earlier; but once again, she found herself being distracted from this.

For the umpteenth time that morning, she saw, Chrissie Telfer was combing her gingery hair, holding the mirror angled so that she could trace every movement of the comb through its strands. But why did she bother so about it? Unwillingly fascinated, Bridie watched the self-regarding performance. It was pretty enough hair in its way, of course, she conceded, fine and crinkly; and so long as there was some light falling on it, it was reasonably attractive. But even so, it hardly seemed to justify the amount of time Chris spent in admiring it. From across the ward, Chris became aware she was being watched, and looked over the edge of the mirror to say complacently:

"I was just lucky, I suppose, to be born with bonny hair."

A sudden commotion at the door of the ward saved Bridie from having to reply to this. Two nurses had entered, escorting between them a woman whose appearance caused a sharp intake of breath from everyone in the ward—a thin woman, barefooted, dressed in a long, drooping skirt and a man's jacket. She was a tinker, Bridie realized—one of the traveling people—and as filthy as tinkers always were. Her feet and legs were black with dirt, and skirt and jacket were blotched with mud and grease. Her hair was a thick, matted mass, dark in color; and dirt had darkened her face also, to the point where it was hard to guess what age she might be.

She was acting like a tinker too, resisting every step of a way that would end in her being penned indoors, struggling with the nurses, cursing and snarling at them. Yet she was an emergency case, Bridie realized as the nurses managed to get the tinker as far as the empty bed next to her own. There was a terrible urgency in the way the nurses kept telling her she must be got into the operating theater as soon as possible. But, they kept insisting also, they could not do that with her until she had been given a bath; and a bath, the cursing voice continued to reply, was the last thing they would get *her* into.

Through the flurry of the nurses' attempts to impose their will on the tinker woman, Bridie became aware of a new figure on the scene—a doctor, stethoscope around his neck, one hand holding a hypodermic syringe. The flurry suddenly calmed. The nurses stepped back. The tinker woman sat on the edge of her bed looking defiantly up at the doctor. The nurses' efforts had succeeded in ridding her of the battered jacket, so that she was dressed now only in the skirt and the dirty fragments of something that might once have been a blouse. The doctor bent towards her, hypodermic at the ready, and said compassionately,

"I'm afraid this may hurt a little."

The tinker woman laughed, a hoarse laugh of such fierce contempt that Bridie felt herself shrinking from the sound. In a voice that matched the laugh, she said,

"Doctor, I'm used to pain."

One swift, scornful gesture, then, and her arm was out-thrust to the needle. Bridie watched the shining point stab into the bare, thin flesh, and wondered how old the tinker woman had been before she started to speak like that—*"I'm used to pain."*

Tinker children were always as ragged and dirty as their parents, but it was different for them with things like pain. No tinker *ever* struck a child. Pain was for when they grew up, for the bloody times when there were bare-knuckle fistfights among the men, and drunken parties where both men and women were all mixed up in the same violent kind of quarreling. But it was still always the women, of course, who got the worst of the beatings in the end—with boots as well as fists, sometimes, and sometimes in an even more brutal way. . . .

Bridie shivered inwardly, remembering the round black tents of the tinker encampment that had appeared periodically beside the village of her childhood, and the night she had been unwilling witness to the sight of a burly tinker man belaboring a slim young woman tinker with a great billet of wood. Uneasily she looked again at the emergency case in the next bed and was relieved to see that the nurses there now had the situation in hand. It was probably the injection that had done the trick, she realized, because the tinker woman now seemed to be too dazed to create trouble for anyone.

"But just you wait till she comes round after her operation," Chris Telfer prophesied once the nurses had wheeled the tinker off to the bathroom. "That's when the sparks will really fly."

There was malice in the way Chris spoke; and malice too in the chatter her comment sparked off among the other patients. Tinks, after all, were thieves and rogues, from the slim young women peddling wooden clothes pegs and slipping shy as deer from door to door to the older women made gross by childbearing but still expert at stealing anything that wasn't actually nailed down. And as for the men, those dark, burly men as strong as their own ponies and always with lean whippet dogs slouching at heel, there wasn't a woman born but would shiver to feel a tinker man's glittering eyes on her. Oh, yes, they were all agreed, the very word "tinker" meant trouble.

They waited for the tink woman to be brought back to the ward, waited with a sort of fearful anticipation for the fulfillment of Chris's prophecy; but the tink disappointed them of the expected yells and curses. She made no sound at all, in fact, once the nurses had brought her back from theater, not even uttering the small cries that always seemed to come from someone recovering consciousness. She did not move, either, once the nurses had tucked the bedcovers firmly around her. Her face, too, remained as still as her body. Yet even so, Bridie found when she opened her eyes on the ward the next morning, Chris had been proved right in a way that no one had expected. And the tinker woman had won her battle with the hospital, after all.

She had gone, silently decamped sometime in the course of the night, leaving only the evidence of her empty bed behind her; and no one could tell how she had managed it. All that the nurses on night shift could do was to stand around exchanging their be-wildered anger at her cunning. All that was left to the day shift coming on duty was the chance to voice a chorus of loud dismay.

"And her with that fresh wound, too," the Day Sister kept exclaiming; while Sister McPherson, her pleasant red face severe for once, spoke disgustedly for the night shift,

"And those *filthy* clothes on top of it!"

The patients in the ward took up where the nurses left off, and chattered even more about the tink than on the previous day; all of them, Bridie noted, except for Chris Telfer. And Chris's silence, she guessed, was not due to the unexpected way she had been proved right. No, sir! There was something else bothering the same Chris, and that was the blow her vanity had suffered when she saw the difference a bath had made in the appearance of the tinker!

Bridie closed her hearing to the gossip of the ward and thought again of the form that had lain stretched in scornful silence on the bed neighboring her own. The tinker woman, she had realized when the nurses brought her back from theater, was quite young. And something else had become evident too, once all the concealing filth had been removed from her. She was beautiful, even though there *had* been an oddly foreign look to the warm brown tones of her skin, the sharply drawn lines of her features. But it was still her hair, that mass of hair the nurses had so carefully lifted clear of the covers, that had dealt the real blow to Chris's vanity!

34

Red, you could have called it, like you could have said the same of the gingery strands that were Chris's pride; but not skimpy like them, and not that flat orangey-red, either. The tinker's hair had been thick, its color a deep, rich auburn, and surrounding her as she lay there it had been like some luxuriant and exotic growth from—

Bridie's racing thoughts stumbled. —*from—from*— from where? Frantically she groped for the word, the phrase, that would aptly finish the sentence in her mind. The foreign-looking appearance of the tinker, that face, so sharp yet so delicate in feature; it could have been the model for a face to be engraved on some long-ago coin, the beautiful face of a princess . . . And that was it! She *had* looked like a Princess—one who had somehow kept her identity secret under dirt and rags; and then, when all that had been stripped from her and her hair also made clean, it was the glory of her hair that had given away the secret of where she had come from. —*from an older land than ours, and from a stranger one.*

With the ending of the tale she had spun for herself flashing triumphantly across her mind at last, Bridie began to consider what form the written version should take, and decided that poetry would suit it best. And meanwhile, her thoughts ran on, the play could wait. Playwriting wasn't really her medium, after all, but verse *was*. She reached for the sheaf of paper in her locker, and then remembered that this was the morning she was due to go home for the start of her convalescence.

"And I'll have all the time I need then to write about the tinker woman," she told herself. Four weeks, the whole of her convalescence, with nothing to do but write! Nothing at all to do except to exploit this latest and most marvelous of the writing experiences the hospital would have given her!

Bridie swung out of bed. Her legs felt weak at first, as weak as they had been on the night the pain had attacked her on the way to Bellwood School. But they soon steadied; and long before she was dressed and ready to go, her mind's eye held a picture of her new poem successfully completed, of the ones she had already given to Mr. Kendall appearing in print at last, and of herself, the author of them all, marching confidently back to work. And so, of course, to even more new experiences that would surely also lead to still more new writing!

5

"So you're back!" they said in the flower shop—skinny old Jemima the First Hand with her pile of dyed black hair and little Bunty the Second Hand with her contrasting head of peroxide blond. Bridie smiled in answer to their smiles of welcome.

"Back on the job," she agreed, and glanced approvingly around the stands of vases. There wasn't a doubt, she thought, that this was the shop at its best; in winter, the time of the really elegant flowers. Long-stemmed hothouse roses and carnations, the first of the mimosa from France . . .

"What about the hospital then?" Jemima interrupted her thought. "How did you get on?"

"All right. Except that the Matron was a snooty old biddy."

"How was she snooty?" Bunty asked, and made great play of haughtily tilting her little snub nose. "Like this?"

They all laughed—even Jemima, much as she disapproved in principle of Bunty's carefree attitudes to life, even stern old Jemima couldn't help laughing then.

"A bit like that," Bridie agreed. "She offered me a job—scrubbing floors!"

"The cheek of her!" Jemima's elderly face quivered with an indignation that threatened to split the mask of makeup she used to disguise her wrinkles. "And you apprenticed to a skilled trade!"

"Oh, hoity-toity!" Bunty mocked, and made an imperious gesture of handing Jemima some of the roses the two of them were unpacking.

"Watch it!" Jemima warned, and turned again to Bridie. "But what brings you back so soon?" she asked. "Your uncle said you'd have four weeks convalescence, and here you are with nearly a week of that still to go."

"Aye," Bunty chimed in. "If the boss says he can do without you till next week, what's *your* hurry?"

What indeed, except the knowledge that the sooner she got back to work, the sooner she'd be sure of the fate of the poems she'd left with Mr. Kendall. Yet how could she risk the laughter of Jemima and Bunty by admitting to this as the urge that had become too strong for her to resist?

With an effort at sounding casual, Bridie repeated the excuse that had persuaded her mother to let her cut short her convalescence, and that had worked also with her Uncle George.

"It was lonely at home in the village with William in school all day and the Others away at their jobs."

Bunty looked a question at this. Bunty was pretty new in the shop—not like Jemima, who had worked so long for Thomas Armstrong & Son that she knew all about every branch of the family.

"William's my young brother," Bridie explained. "And the Others are my sisters—three of them, all older than me."

Jemima added, showing off her knowledge, "And they're called 'the Others,' see, because Bridie was always her daddy's favorite. Or so her mammy told me, anyway." She stooped to take the last of the roses from their box, and straightened up to add, "And talking of your mammy, Bridie, it's a long time since I've seen her. How is she, these days?"

"Oh, she's fine. Fine, thanks, Jemima."

"I'm glad to hear it. Because she's been through some terrible times, after all, since your dad died."

"Hey!" Bunty attracted attention with a quick gesture towards the van just drawing up outside the shop window. "There's the boss," she said warningly. "Time to get the skates on, girls!"

The three of them scattered: Jemima to put the vase of roses onto one of the stands, Bunty to clear away the emptied box, Bridie to fetch the flowered overall that was her working dress. Her Uncle George came in, followed by Hughie, the van driver.

Hughie was the rough, tough kind of young man

that Edinburgh contemptuously called a "keelie." He was small, his growth stunted by the slum life of the High Street. A mat of curly hair and eyes gleaming above the squint line of a broken nose were all that could be seen behind the load of potted hyacinths he carried. But Hughie was strong; and in spite of being a keelie, he always had a sort of cocky cheerfulness about him. He winked at Bridie, set his load down without effort, and said in his hoarse, street-ruffian voice,

"Aye aye, hen. Y'r lookin' grand!"

Jemima began checking the number of pots, while Uncle George said, "There's another three hundred to come, Jemima, on top of this lot. Push the sale as hard as you can. And, Bridie"—one hand beckoning drew Bridie with him into the back shop—"you can moss for me while I make up. That'll keep you on a sitting-down job for the first wee while back at work."

A pile of wire wreath frames, the moss to pad these, the twine to bind the moss, were all lying ready in the back shop. And, it seemed, the order book that morning was a good one. But it usually was, of course, in winter. Winter was the time of old people dying. But still, according to Uncle George, it was an ill wind that blew nobody good, because winter was also the time when flowers were most expensive; and if a flower shop couldn't make a good profit out of *that* situation, it would never make one at all.

Bridie lifted her first handful of moss with the beginning of a chant learned in childhood coming into her mind. *When you see a hearse go by, d'you ever think*

40

you're going to die. It was sphagnum moss she had to work with, thank goodness. Sphagnum was always clean—not like the carpet moss that so often had worms in the earth clinging to it. *They put you in a long white shirt, and cover you up with heaps of dirt.* Sphagnum was the stuff they had used to pad field dressings in the Great World War, when it hadn't been possible to get cotton wool. She could remember her mother telling her so. *The worms crawl in, the worms crawl out; they crawl in thin and come out stout—*

Uncle George had taken a prepared wreath frame and was already halfway through his first wreath. White of Harrisii lilies, red of carnations—those were the colors he had chosen, white and red, the colors of death . . . *since your dad died . . .*

"Stop it!" Bridie told herself firmly. "*Stop* thinking of things that make you remember Dad. You promised yourself you would."

Without taking his eyes off his wreath, her uncle remarked, "You're very quiet this morning."

He was working fast, as he always did, a wing of his dark hair falling untidily forward, right hand flashing out to the trays of florists' wire and back again to the flower held ready in his left. A quick move then, to make wire and flower stem lie parallel, a series of expert twists that bound part of the wire around the stem, a jabbing action that forced the wire's free end through the moss on the frame—and there was yet another bloom positioned in the pattern of white and red.

"I was watching you," Bridie excused herself.

41

Now he did glance at her. "That's a change. When you're quiet it usually means you've gone off into another of your daydreams." He put the finishing touches to his wreath, stepped back to judge the effect, and then turned to tell her, "I've been thinking about you. You'll need shorter hours at the shop for the next week or so. And your granny says you've to go early to bed, which means you'll have to cut out night school too for a while."

"But my work—" In dismay at this blow to her plans for seeing Mr. Kendall, Bridie began her protest, and was cut short by her uncle saying flatly,

"Your work lies here. And don't argue with me, because getting your strength back is the duty you owe it."

He lifted the wreath from the table that was his workbench, slid it to the floor and moved to the doorway of the back shop calling for Jemima to bring him some roses. His actions gave Bridie time to invent an excuse that might counter the blow, and immediately she put this to the test.

"My teacher—I have a book he loaned me. And I'm already overdue to return it. I'll have to go down to Bellwood for that."

"Okay." Uncle George turned from taking Jemima's burden of roses. "Just don't loiter when you get there, that's all. Now look. I'm going to show you the trick of wiring these roses so that the petals can't fall. You take a hair-thin wire—a number twelve. See? And you do like so. . . ."

With a quick thrust he sent the fine wire through

the head of the rose in his left hand. Talking still, his stubby fingers moving with surprising delicacy, he wove the free end of the wire invisibly through the petals of the rose.

"There!" He handed Bridie the finished effort. "Watch me do the others for this wreath; but keep that one for a model and practice from it whenever you have a minute."

Bridie put the wired rose-head in water, and the making up went on until the floor of the back shop was covered with finished wreaths. Hughie came in then to help Uncle George load them into the van. Bunty put the kettle on for tea, and Jemima poked up the fire in the back shop. Hughie drove off to deliver the wreaths, and Uncle George hurried back to where the rest of them sat with feet stretched out to the blaze and cups of hot tea clasped between numb hands. Cold, perpetual cold in feet and hands, was the penalty they had to pay for the atmosphere needed to keep the flowers fresh; and in wintertime especially, they all needed this morning break.

"Come on then, Bridie," Jemima said. "Tell us more about that hospital. I bet you saw a bit of life there, eh?"

She laughed as she spoke, and glanced at Uncle George with the kind of look Bridie had come to recognize in the adults of her world. To dislike also, because it meant they were slyly trying to discover how much she might have learned about the supposedly secret things of *their* world. And when her uncle grinned at the remark, when he flashed Jemima the same kind of look in answer to it, Bridie thought she knew exactly what the two of them were signaling to one another.

Little Miss Innocent won't be so innocent now, will she?

And yet, her thoughts ran resentfully on, they would still expect her to pretend to be innocent. They always did, because they'd be shocked out of their stupid minds if someone her age admitted to being anything else. And that, of course, was what allowed them to play this game with her, this teasing game where they never seemed to realize she could guess at the smutty thoughts they were having about her. And where she couldn't hold her own against the teasing *except* by acting the part they expected her to play.

"We-e-ll," she began slowly, and saw how her reluctance had immediately made them all grin with anticipation. Her resentment flared; and made bold by the force of it, she suddenly found herself breaking all the unspoken rules of the game.

"There was this fat woman," she said. "Liz, they called her. She was fifty-one and still having her periods. But she hadn't read the right books, and so she was dead scared of her husband giving her another baby."

Jemima and Uncle George both looked as if they had suddenly bitten on a lemon. Bunty's face had a sort of astonished approval on it, but Uncle George was making the throat-clearing sound that was a prelude to reproof, and Bunty wouldn't risk raising her voice against that. *She* would, though, Bridie thought.

They'd asked for it—Jemima and her Uncle George. They'd damn well asked for it.

"But Fat Liz wasn't the kind to let herself be beat by all that." Rapidly she pressed on over the sound of her uncle's first words. "And so the next time this doctor—Dr. Johnson—came to the ward . . ."

She was safely launched now into the full version of the Drama of the Tubes, with enjoyment at having taken command of the situation adding its own impetus to the telling, making Fat Liz once more vivid before her mind's eye; Fat Liz in the full importance of her dilemma, Fat Liz boldly announcing her decision, and then keeping the whole ward agog with curiosity over the interview with Dr. Johnson. The tones of the woman's voice began to creep into her own voice; and at that, she noted, there were smiles on the three faces watching her. She enlarged the performance by allowing her gestures to become those Fat Liz had made, and the smiles grew broader.

"Oh, my dear!" With the drama reaching its crisis, Bridie leaned forward to stretch her arms in imitation of Liz showing herself cradled by Dr. Johnson. "Oh, my *dear*," she repeated. "If I had but known—" A pause then, as Liz herself had paused to give emphasis to the final line of the drama—but also to relish again for their own sake the tragicomedy of the words; and then, with all the heartfelt flourish Liz had imparted to them, "I'd have *cut the tubes!*"

Laughter, a burst of laughter from all three of her listeners, was the reward of her effort, and triumphantly she sat back to enjoy it. But her uncle sobered

45

before the other two did, and disapproval had crept back into the voice that said,

"Well, you have to live and learn, I suppose, Bridie. But a young girl like you still has no right to be making free with a coarse story like that."

"She told it well." Jemima, at least, was still grinning. "You have to say that for her."

Uncle George shrugged. "She got the gift from her mother."

"Aye." Jemima nodded. "I remember the way your sister talked from the time you were both kids. And Bridie, here, is every bit as good at acting out a story as she ever was."

"And looks well on it too!" a voice cried heartily from the doorway of the back shop. "As well as ever."

It was Henry, from J & K Mathews, Funeral Directors, coming in pat on Jemima's final words. Henry always spoke in a hearty voice. Henry always smelled too, of mothballs and of the queer, musty odor of the funeral parlor. Henry had big meaty hands and thick meaty lips. Henry was a— Bridie caught Bunty's eye on her, saw Bunty's mouth silently shaping a word, and looked hastily away again. Yet stubbornly still, her mind persisted in adding Bunty's word to her own unfinished sentence. Henry was a grope; those disgustingly meaty hands always trying to touch, to pat, to caress. Henry was everything she couldn't bear to have near her. But Henry was also a hard worker, a regular churchgoer. Henry, in her uncle's opinion at least, was therefore a very worthy young man. Besides which, of course, it was policy for Uncle George to be on good terms with

46

anyone in the funeral business. And so she smiled when he smiled at Henry kindly asking if she felt as well as she looked, and politely she answered,

"Yes indeed, thank you, Henry."

"But we mustn't work her too hard yet, eh, Mr. Armstrong?" Henry was still only nineteen, but that didn't stop him being shrewd enough to know that Uncle George had him marked out as an up-and-coming funeral director. Jovially, but still with just the right hint of deference to someone much older than himself, he boomed out his question, and hastily Uncle George agreed,

"No, no, of course not. I was planning for her to leave early today, in fact."

"Fine! Then I'll give her my strong right arm back to her Granny's house—with your permission of course, Mr. Armstrong."

Behind Uncle George's back, Bunty's lips formed another word. *Creep!* As if she didn't know that Henry was also a creep! But there was Uncle George expressing appreciation of so gallant an offer. There was Henry himself earning even more of her uncle's approval by saying no, no, he was too busy for a cup of tea, but thank you all the same, Jemima. And what could *she* do in the face of all that?

"You're not so dumb as I thought you were," Bunty said when the end of teatime found only herself and Bridie in the back shop. "And so I'm telling you, that creep Henry has his eye on you, and it's time you did something about it."

"Such as?"

"Bawl him out. That's my advice. Give him a good *sherickin'*."

Bridie shrugged. It was all very well for Bunty to talk like that. Bunty wasn't far removed from the keelie girls that went around with Hughie. And you had to be as tough as the keelies before you could demolish anyone with the barrage of gutter language they called a sherickin'.

"It's true, though," Bunty insisted. "They can't take a sherickin', mealymouths like him. And he wouldn't hang around for another, I can tell you. Or what about this?" She clenched her right hand into a fist and punched the air. "Bunch o' fives, eh? You could get your fella to do that for you—give creepy Henry a bunch o' fives, right smack in the kisser!"

"I could, I suppose," Bridie agreed, "except that I haven't got a fella."

Bunty was supposed to be washing out flower vases. Now she deserted the sink completely, seized a towel to dry her hands and then stood thoughtfully primping up the permanent wave in her peroxide-blond hair.

"That," she began slowly, "isn't the way *I* heard it, because"—she stopped, grinned suddenly, and then finished in a rush—"because the Sister on your ward told your granny and your granny told Jemima and Jemima told me that your fella came to the hospital to visit you. *And*, the Sister said, it was the way the two of you looked at one another that made her sure he *is* your fella."

"He's not! I mean—"

"Ah ha!" With a last triumphant pat at the Jean Harlow hairdo, Bunty pounced. "So it's true! You *did* have a fella come to visit you."

"Oh, shut up!" In a flush of annoyance at the way she had allowed the situation to trap her into admission of the visit, Bridie banged her wreath frame down on the table. "His name's Peter McKinley, if you must know, and he's *not* my fella. He's just someone in my class at night school."

"M-hmm." Bunty wasn't convinced. "But there must be other chaps in that class, and they didn't visit you."

"He was the one that had the sense to call an ambulance for me."

"Oh, aye? And was all smiles when he came to see you—according to the Sister, at least. And you were all smiles back at him."

But why shouldn't she have smiled with pleasure at the unexpectedness of Peter's visit? "I didn't know he would—" The look of avid curiosity on Bunty's face interrupted Bridie's answer. Talk about "fellas" was meat and drink to Bunty, she warned herself, and there would be yet more teasing to come if she went on talking about Peter's visit.

'Bunty!" Jemima's voice sounded from the front shop; and then again, with irritation in it, "Will you hurry up with those fresh vases!"

Bunty turned hastily to fill her vases with water; and to Bridie's great relief when that job was finished, she was left alone in the back shop.

6

In the lights that went on early because of the short-
ness of the winter day, the front shop had taken on
the gleam of an Aladdin's cave of color: deep red and
white and golden of the big shaggy-headed chrysanthemums, purple of anemones, yellow of mimosa, ce-
rise and silver-pink of roses, with the rainbow hues
of the delicate little freesia blossoms echoing the colors
of all the other flowers. It was the aspect of the shop
that had always most intrigued Bridie; and always
also, it fascinated her to see how it attracted people
in from the dark of the world outside.

Uncle George had gone off on a big decorating job—
a flower display in the Music Hall in George Street.
But he had said she could serve that afternoon if she
felt up to all the running around, and the shop was

certainly busy enough to justify Jemima calling on her help. She joined the other two there and as usual then, she found it easy to predict who would buy what.

Old ladies, and children looking for a present for a grown-up, were the ones who bought the cheapest flowers—the small pot plants or bunches of the sturdy little anemones. Well-dressed, matronly women always chose the big, expensive chrysanthemums that would doubtless then be displayed in drawing rooms as opulent as their owners. As for the roses and carnations, it was nearly always men who bought those—dashing young men who wanted to sport a flower in a buttonhole, shy young men carefully selecting as many as they could afford to present to a girl friend, fat and prosperous-looking men who lavished cigar smoke around the shop while they called for the biggest and most expensive of bouquets. And men like Mr. Finkelstein, of course, who took a modest bunch of roses home once a week without fail to his wife.

Mr. Finkelstein was the jeweler from down the street, and he came in that afternoon demanding, in his German-sounding voice, that it must be Bridie who served him.

"Because I have heard from young Henry that you are well again, *mein Liebling*. And for Mrs. Finkelstein, always you choose the nicest, the best of your roses. Also because you are pretty with your blond hair and your eyes so gray-green like the *Nordsee*—yourself like a little Scottish rose—*nicht?*"

Jemima and Bunty stood hiding their smiles at the way Mr. Finkelstein spoke; and behind his back, she knew, they were calling him scornful names like *Yid* and *Ikey Mo.* The fulsome compliments he always paid her were embarrassing too, but she didn't terribly mind that. Granda Armstrong and Mr. Finkelstein were such old friends, after all, that she had become quite accustomed to the experience. She rather liked Mr. Finkelstein, in fact, and it was maybe this, she thought, that made her feel he was only acting his usual breeziness with her that day. Then Granda Armstrong himself came in, as he did every day at four o'clock to check the takings against those in his other shop; and Mr. Finkelstein's manner changed so much that she knew she had been right in her feeling. A look passed between him and her grandfather, then Granda Armstrong asked quietly,

"Any news yet, from Germany?"

Mr. Finkelstein nodded, the smile gone from his face, leaving the lines of it tight and drawn instead. Very low, he answered,

"Yes. I know for certain now that my brother is dead."

Granda Armstrong gave a shocked exclamation. "How?" he asked. "What happened?"

"His shop—" Mr. Finkelstein began and swallowed hard. Bridie thought, *Maybe I'm not supposed to hear this.* But she was trapped between the two men, with neither of them seeming to notice her standing there still waiting to hand Mr. Finkelstein his roses.

"His shop," Mr. Finkelstein began again, "was attacked by a gang of Hitler Brownshirts—Nazis. They smashed and burned everything in it: all his beautiful pictures, his glass, his silver. Then they dragged my brother into the street and they—they beat him to death. My sister-in-law escaped to Switzerland, and from there she has written to me of this. She saw it all. My brother's children too. They saw it."

"Merciful God!" Granda Armstrong stared in horror. "I'm sorry. Finkelstein, old friend, I can't say how sorry I am. It's—it's— Such barbarity! It's almost unbelievable!"

Mr. Finkelstein rubbed wearily at his face, as if trying to wipe the haggard look from it. "Nevertheless, my friend, it is still only Europe running true to past form. Does a people need a scapegoat for its troubles? They pick on the Jews. One by one at first, they are killed. And then comes the mass murder—the pogrom. It has all happened many times before this."

"But that *is* all in the past," Granda Armstrong protested. "And surely, surely, there should be no room for such uncivilized ideas in this day and age."

Mr. Finkelstein made a blind clutch for the roses in Bridie's hand. "Friend Armstrong," he said bitterly, "do not tell that to me. Tell it to Herr Adolf Hitler."

When Mr. Finkelstein had gone, Granda Armstrong began to count the till. Bridie picked up his cane, the gold-topped one he always carried, and went to put it safely in the back shop, glad of the excuse this gave her to be on her own. She laid the cane carefully on the table and sat beside it, staring at a tormenting inner vision of a man lying battered to death in a street in Germany. Before the very eyes of his wife and children, too. And just because he was Jewish!

53

Supposing it had been *her* father—but no! Suppose anything but that. Bad enough that Dad was dead, without imagining that additional horror! Just think of Germany instead. Germany . . . What did she know about the people there? Dad had liked them—and that had been in spite of his having had to spend two miserable years in one of their Prisoner of War camps in the Great World War. They were sensible people, he had told her. Religious, too; and he had respected them for that, even although he hadn't been a religious man himself. Yet how did they square their treatment of Jews with worship of a Jewish God? And where had all the hatred started? How had it been possible for this man, Hitler, to whip it on to the point of murder? Because of scornful names like Yid and Ikey Mo—had the beginning been as simple as that?

There must be books that would explain it for her, Bridie decided. She would hunt them out, read about it for herself. But meanwhile . . .

There were words coming into her head, a rhythmic sequence of words that would express something of this bewildered outrage against the obscenity that had been the death of Mr. Finkelstein's brother. With one hand, she drew towards her a scrap of green wrapping paper lying beside her grandfather's cane. With the other, she picked up the pencil from the order book and began to set down the words in the pattern their rhythm demanded.

If Christ came down from Calvary
And found he was a Yid,

54

Would that make news?
What would they say in Germany?

"Bridie . . ." It was Granda Armstrong interrupting her train of thought, briefly acknowledging her presence in the back shop before he placed himself in front of the fire with coattails lifted so that the heat of it could reach his backside. She watched him, waiting for him to speak again.

He still had his glossy black top hat on, and everything he wore was in keeping with it: black tailcoat, black-and-white-striped trousers, pearl-gray waistcoat with a heavy gold watch chain looped across it, and pearl-gray spats over his high-polished black boots. His face was ruddy from the cold outside, and he was frowning, one hand raised now to stroke the white of his small, pointed beard.

"Mr. Finkelstein," he said, "forgot to pay you for his roses."

She nodded. "Will I mark it in the book against him?"

"Yes. Trade is trade, no matter what happens."

He reached for the big gold watch at the end of its chain, flipped it open, and studied its face. *Trade is trade.* It was a hard dictum, Bridie thought. But hadn't he and his family—her own mother excepted, of course—hadn't they always been hard where money was concerned? *Trade is trade.* They were a hard lot altogether, the merchants of Edinburgh. And proud of themselves for that, too! A memory flickered somewhere in her mind and suddenly became clear.

It had been in one of the books she had studied in the National Library, a description of the long-ago merchants of Edinburgh, so proud of their status in the city that they'd flaunted it by carrying gold-topped canes and dressing always in scarlet velvet; and what she was seeing now, she realized, was not just her granda who always insisted on wearing such formal clothes. This old man was also the embodiment of a tradition. He was Thomas Armstrong, Merchant of Edinburgh, dressed in a way that would inform everyone of his status, and—right down to the constant presence of his gold-topped cane—would display the pride he took in it.

The watch clicked shut. Granda Armstrong said, "George seems to be running late with that Music Hall job." His gaze fastened on Bridie's scrap of green wrapping paper, the pencil she held half-poised over it, and abruptly he asked, "And you? What are you up to? Is that more of the scribbling you're always doing?"

Scribbling! Bridie put her hand defensively flat over the paper. It was the same everywhere; even at home when she had tried so hard to write her verse drama about the tink woman. Even there her mother had used the same slighting word about her efforts.

"It was just a thought," she muttered. "I wrote it down to remember it."

"You think too much," her grandfather told her. "And you're very pale, all of a sudden. A lassie your age has no right to be pale-faced."

"It's my first day back at work, Granda. I'm just a bit tired, that's all."

Granda Armstrong's frowning expression changed to one of concern. "Then why's your uncle keeping you here?"

"He's not. He said I could go early. I'm just waiting till he comes back from the decorating job."

"No need. No need at all for that." Granda Armstrong began moving towards the front shop. "I'll tell Jemima so while you get your coat on."

And if I go now I'll escape Henry! The thought came quickly to Bridie's mind, but she was too late with it, after all. To her disgust, as she reached for her coat, she heard the booming notes of Henry's voice coming from the front shop. She pocketed her few lines of poetry to the sound of him talking to her grandfather in the same way as he talked to Uncle George: heartily, piously, making himself out to be oh such an upright young man! And Granda, of course, was just as fooled by that as Uncle George always was—more so, in fact, because Uncle George wasn't really religious at heart. But Granda was! Granda believed every single word in the Bible, and it would never occur to him to doubt anyone who quoted it the way Henry did!

Yet even so, Bridie asked herself dolefully as she went towards the two of them, why was it still only girls who could see what a creep Henry really was?

7

Henry talked all the way home, gripping Bridie by the elbow and steering her masterfully through the shoppers crowding the lamp-lit street.

First of all it was about how well he was doing with J & K Mathews, Funeral Directors. Then it was about all the gossip of the other shops in the street—including the newest of that, the death of Mr. Finkelstein's brother. A sad business, that had been, Henry declared. Not that he had much time himself, of course, for old Ikey Mo Finkelstein. But that sort of thing was going too far, especially considering the fact that the Jews had once been—and here Henry's voice grew reverent, as it always did when he quoted the Bible— God's chosen people. On the other hand, they'd gone and spoiled it all for themselves—hadn't they?—when they had rejected Christ as the Messiah. And so it was quite likely that the way matters were in Germany now was just an expression of God's will, after all.

God's will! Bridie's hand closed tightly over her scrap of green wrapping paper, and through clenched teeth she said:

"You're a hypocrite, Henry. A dyed-in-the-wool hypocrite."

Henry laughed. "Don't be silly, now," he reproved her. "You know you can't make me angry, Bridie, because I'm a Christian and I'll always turn the other cheek."

In other words, Bridie thought, there's no argument will make an impression on *you*! Deliberately after that, she closed her ears to the sound of the voice droning at her side and tried to ignore the fact of the meaty grasp on her elbow. At the corner of Cluny Road and Comiston Crescent, however, she became once more alert. This was the danger time, once they had turned away from the lights of Cluny and were into the darker section of road running from there to her grandparents' house in Comiston. With all her senses now stretched to take account of this, she became aware also of Henry telling her:

". . . and as you know, Bridie, it's my considered view that cinemas are sinful places, and I would never normally dream of setting foot in one. But this film—*Green Pastures*, it was called—was supposed to be a film of the Gospel Story. And so I thought it was my duty to go, my bounden duty. But would you believe it, all the actors were *black*—black as the ace of spades,

59

every last one of them—including the one that played God!"

"Well?" She glanced up at him. "What's wrong with that? Just tell me, Henry, what's wrong with a black man being an actor? It's a job, isn't it, just like any other job?"

"What's wrong with it!" Henry's indignation sent the pitch of his voice soaring. "It's bad enough, isn't it, for any man to presume to impersonate God? But for a black man to do that—it was blasphemy, the sheerest blasphemy!"

"How on earth," she demanded, "do you make that out? If you believe your God is—" Abruptly she checked the rest of her challenge. They had reached the gate to her grandmother's garden, she realized, and was annoyed with herself for having been drawn into an argument that would now give Henry an excuse for lingering there. She made to turn to the gate, but his hands on her shoulders prevented the turn.

"Listen!" he was telling her. "Black people are all very well in their own way, of course, and we've got to feel sorry for them because they're black. But that doesn't mean we should let them get away with that kind of thing. And you'll find plenty besides me to tell you so. So just you stop talking from the depth of your ignorance, my girl, or—" A thick note came into his voice, his grasp on her shoulders tightened. "—Or I'll have to teach you better!"

"That'll be the day! When *you* educate *me!*"

"Oh, come on, now! You're a girl, aren't you? And I've yet to meet the girl who can think straight."

"Henry—" She was afraid suddenly of the way he had begun to lean in to her, and disgusted by the musty, funeral-parlor smell coming from him. Anger against him fought with the fear and disgust, but still she managed to keep enough control to say coldly, "Let go of me, Henry. You're supposed to be a Christian, remember? One of the good and pure of the earth."

"Even when I'm tempted?" Henry's voice grew thicker yet. "As good men always have been tempted, ever since Adam . . ."

Bridie made a swift calculation. She wasn't strong enough to break Henry's grip. But maybe, if she took a leaf out of Bunty's book, she could shock him into letting her go. With fierce energy, she thrust both hands against his chest and snarled,

"Geroff, ya lousy nyaff! Away and hurl yer barra!"

He fell back from her, his mouth a gape of astonishment. "What? What did you say?"

"You heard me." Hands on hips, as she had seen Bunty stand, Bridie struck a swaggering pose. "Whadda ya use yer ears fur—ornaments?"

"But that's keelie talk, that's—"

"Ach, shut yer Holy Willie gob before I get ma fella tae kick yer teeth in. And if ya want a damned sight more o' a sherickin', just you try layin' yer dirty mitts on *me* again!"

She swung away from the appalled look on his face, crashed open the garden gate, and raced up the path to the front door of the house. Her grandmother's voice called to her seconds after she had closed the door behind her, and breathlessly she called back:

61

"Yes, it's me. Granda let me off early. But I'm going up to rest before tea."

She rushed upstairs, her mind still convulsed with fury at Henry; Henry's loathsome caresses, Henry's damnable condescension to her. *I've yet to meet the girl who can think straight.* How dared he! And his hypocrisy over the thugs who had murdered Mr. Finkelstein's brother, his pious outrage over a black actor playing *his* God—how dared he make canting excuses for the one, and so loftily despise the other!

With the door of her room swinging violently shut behind her, Bridie fished the scrap of green wrapping paper from her pocket. Her voice shaking, she read aloud the first line on it. *If Christ came down from Calvary* . . . If God were black— But that was the beginning of a new verse! It had to be—damn Henry's eyes! Reaching for a pencil and a book on which to rest her paper, Bridie sat down and wrote:

*If God were black, would white men praise
Or would they curse his name?
And when they sang,
What hymns of hatred would they raise?*

It wasn't so good as the first verse, she thought. And there had been hesitations, a lot of them, and many scratchings-out too, before she reached the final form. But she had succeeded in keeping the rhythm. It still flowed. A last spurt of her fury at Henry urged her to try a third verse. *If God were female* . . . The opening words of it leapt immediately to her mind. She wrote them down, smiling grimly to herself, and the rest of the verse followed easily on.

If God were female, would there then
Be swift mass exodus
Through Heaven's gate?
Or would the exiles all be men?

Now there had to be something final, something that would tie these two new verses to the first she had written; because Henry's self-righteousness was no different from the cruelty she had been tilting at then. Henry, in fact—she could see it clearly now—was just a type, the kind who was always despising, always hating, always smugly justifying himself for the way he kept renewing the pains of Calvary. . . .

Bridie looked up and saw the reflection in the mirror on the opposite wall—her own face, her image, staring out at her. Words began to move again in her mind, words suddenly springing clear of all the biblical study that had been required of her in childhood. . . . *in the image of God, made he man. . . .* Her face, yes; but *her* image? She looked away from the questioning stare in the mirrored eyes, and once more began to write.

If I were you, and you were I,
Would each in each perceive
God's image stamped?
Would we admit it, or deny?

Oh mirror, mirror on the wall!
God dies again, each time

63

You fail to show
To each of us, the face of all.

She had copied the poem out, with the title *Mirror, Mirror* . . . neatly printed above it. And now she was running again, running through the dark of Bellwood Road, even though there was no need for her to hurry. *Habit!* Bridie grinned to herself at the thought and changed her pace to a fast walk.

The book that was to be her excuse for seeing Mr. Kendall was clutched under her left arm. Her right hand, thrust deep into her coat pocket, was curled around the paper with the new poem on it; and already in her mind she was discussing this with Mr. Kendall, asking him if he thought it might be good enough to add to those she had already given him to read. But she had plenty of time yet to reach the school before his class had the ten-minute break that would allow the two of them the chance to talk.

Bellwood Hall again, and people dancing . . . That snooty matron had been right about one thing, at least. It hadn't really taken long for her to recover from the operation. She, too, could now dance—if anybody asked her. And *if* she could somehow learn the kind of dancing they did at the Bellwood.

On her way through the school gates, Bridie took a final glance at the time shown in the lit clock tower. Twenty-eight minutes past eight, and it would take her two minutes to reach Mr. Kendall's room—everything was going exactly as she had planned. She hurried down the drive, into the entrance hall, and up the two flights of stairs leading to the Language classrooms.

At the head of the first flight she was caught up in a surge of the students who had poured out of her own class in Advanced English. Peter McKinley was among those who smiled at her and would have stopped to speak, but she had only ten minutes to see Mr. Kendall, after all, and there would be plenty of time after that.

"Later," she told Peter hurriedly. "I've got to rush now, but I'll see you later."

Breathless, she reached her classroom, and pushed open the door.

There was a strange man sitting at Mr. Kendall's desk. He looked up at her entrance, frowning a little, and said abruptly,

"Yes? Who are you?"

"I wanted—I mean, I'm—" Bridie floundered about, grasping at words. "I'm one of Mr. Kendall's students, sir."

"Are you?" The strange man's frown deepened. "I wasn't aware he had any as young as you seem to be."

"He hasn't. Not usually, anyway. I got special permission from the Headmaster to take his class."

"I see. And now?"

"Well, I've been absent for a while. I wanted to talk to him about something, and I—"

She stopped. The strange man was shaking his head at her as if she had made some kind of blunder.

"Not possible now, I'm afraid," he told her. "Mr. Kendall is no longer on the staff of the school. But

I've taken over his work here, and if I can help you . . ."

He left the offer hanging on the air, waiting for her to speak, but all she could do was to stand there like a fool, gaping at him. And clearly, he was a man who had no time for fools. With a little grunt of impatience, he looked back towards the papers on his desk.

"But where's Mr. Kendall now?" In her confusion, Bridie shot the question with a force she had not intended. The strange man turned his head to glare angrily at her before he snapped,

"How should I know that?"

Seconds later she was out of the classroom and hurrying back downstairs, with only the vaguest recollection of how she had reached that point. But one thing *was* clear in her mind. The School Secretary was bound to know where Mr. Kendall was now. She had to see the School Secretary.

In the entrance hall, students milled around barring her way to the Secretary's office. Peter McKinley was among them. He waved to her again and called out, but this time she was too agitated even to acknowledge his greeting. Head down, she bored determinedly through the press, knocked on the Secretary's door, and was on the other side of it without waiting for an answer to her knock.

"Where's Mr. Kendall? I want to see Mr. Kendall."

The sour look her entrance had caused became even sourer. "Do you, now!" The Secretary sat back in her chair, looking Bridie up and down. She was a fat woman. The chair creaked under her weight. Her little eyes lying deep-creased behind her spectacles were

66

narrowed in displeasure, and hastily Bridie tried to retrieve the blunder that had so evidently set the woman against her.

"Look, I'm sorry I burst in like that. I'm supposed to be off sick, you see, but I wanted to talk to Mr. Kendall. And he's not here. There was another man who said he wasn't on the staff anymore."

A brusque nod from the Secretary. "That's right. He's got another job—a shift up the ladder."

"Well, then—" Hesitantly, Bridie tried again. "I just thought—that is, I wondered if you could tell me where he is now."

Nervously she waited for an answer. The woman, she thought, looked like a Hereford cow—little eyes, short, frizzy hair, jowly face. And why should *she* now be shaking her head?

"You students," the Secretary said contemptuously, "you need your backsides skelped, you do, the way you chase after the men on the staff. And it's no part of *my* job to help you with that."

She bent to her desk again. Bridie stood trying to choke down her anger at the insult. When she thought she could trust her voice not to shake, she said,

"Listen, you've got it wrong. Mr. Kendall had something belonging to me—some homework. I want it back, that's all."

The Secretary looked up. "You could have said that at the beginning, couldn't you?" Ponderously she bent sideways to open a drawer of her desk. "What's your name?"

"McShane. Bridie McShane."

Fingers scrabbling in the drawer, the Secretary muttered to herself. She straightened up, a familiar-looking buff envelope in her hand. "This has your name on it."

Bridie stretched out a clutching hand. The envelope *was* the one she had used for the poems she had given Mr. Kendall. She freed herself from her book, dropping it onto the Secretary's desk, and ripped the envelope open. The folded sheets that bore her poems were there, exactly as they had been before—just those, and nothing else; not a line, not a single scrape of the pen to say what Mr. Kendall had thought of them.

"Well?" The Secretary's voice came sharply through her daze of disappointment. "You've got what you wanted, haven't you?"

Bridie looked up. "Yes, these belong to me, but I— Look, when did Mr. Kendall leave?"

"Three weeks—no, nearer four weeks ago. As soon as he'd worked out the notice he had to give here."

"But—" *Four weeks ago! That would be just about a week after she'd been taken to hospital.* The Secretary was staring.

"But what?"

Through the bewilderment fogging her brain, Bridie heard herself say stupidly, "He never told me he was leaving."

Still those little eyes staring, but suspicious now. "Why should he? He's a teacher, for God's sake. Why should he discuss his career prospects with a student?"

Why, indeed! Yet he must have known he would be

68

changing jobs, long before she gave him the poems. And he'd known, too, how much she'd been looking forward to the chance of having some of them published. And still he'd gone off to his new job without writing her a single word about them.

Slowly Bridie began stuffing the envelope of poems into her coat pocket. *Callous! That's what he was. Just downright callous.* She turned away from the desk, muttering a formula of thanks to the Secretary. The woman's voice called her back.

"Hey! Your book!"

In silence, Bridie retrieved the book and once more made for the door. From the entrance hall outside it she heard an echoing tread that told of students returning to their upper-floor classrooms; but the hall itself was deserted now, except for a solitary figure lingering beside the staircase. Bridie averted her face and walked quickly to the door, pretending she had not recognized Peter McKinley as the figure at the foot of the stairs.

"Bridie! Wait!" Quickly he intercepted her course and pulled her to a halt. "What's the trouble? Why all the rushing about? Is there—"

"Let go!" Straining against his hold on her right arm, she interrupted the questions. "I can't talk to you just now."

"Why not? What have I done?"

"Nothing. I know I said I'd see you later, but now I just don't want to talk. Not to anyone."

"Bridie—" He tugged at her arm, trying to turn her to face him. "There *is* something wrong. Or you

69

wouldn't be tearing around here like you've been doing tonight when you're still supposed to be convalescing at home. Would you?"

"Please!" She kept her face away, resisting as much as possible his efforts to see it. "I know you've been very decent to me, but it's still not anything you can help."

"You can't know that till you try." His hold on her tightened. "And you'll feel better, you know, if you do spill it out."

He had her half turned to face him now, and she could feel herself weakening. There was something very nice about him, after all. There had to be, seeing he had taken the trouble to visit her in hospital—not to mention what she owed him for calling that ambulance. And anyway, it probably would be a relief to talk to him, *if* she could get words past the great ball of misery choking in her throat. She opened her mouth to speak, but in the split second of doing so, a question flashed into her mind.

Supposing Mr. Kendall had left no note for her because her poetry was so damned bad it just wasn't worth a comment?

Humiliation burned through her, and she cringed from the feeling. She could not bear it, she cried inwardly. And not for another second, either, could she bear to be held there in danger of betraying herself into speaking of it. With her mind fleeing into the refuge of anger, she shouted,

"I *told* you to let me go!"

As the words left her mouth she swung upwards

with her free hand, not caring where the blow landed so long as it freed her from the need to stand there enduring her humiliation. But that, she had forgotten, was the hand holding her book. Its hard edge struck Peter McKinley's face, and although she gasped with remorse even as the blow landed, she could not take it back again.

He made no sound after the first involuntary cry it drew from him. Only the hurt astonishment in his eyes reproached her. She backed a step, too sick with sudden self-loathing to utter a word, then turned and ran out into the night with the shame of her action snarling like a pack of devils at her heels.

8

In the backwash of gloom from the brief, disastrous visit to Bellwood School, Bridie found the atmosphere of her grandparents' house even more oppressive than it usually seemed to her.

It wasn't so bad, she thought, when she could escape to her own room in the attic story. There was real solitude up there among all the other empty rooms that had once held the children of her mother's generation and the servants of Granda's heyday as a merchant; and solitude meant the chance to brood, and brood again over all the possible reasons for Mr. Kendall rejecting her poems *without even saying why*! Up there in the attic story, too, she could relive the scene with Peter McKinley and make it come out the way it ought to have come out, with her having the courage to stand her ground so that she could explain and apologize, with Peter forgiving her, and with both of them then quite happily agreeing that Kendall was no real critic of poetry anyway. But down below the attic story was a very different matter.

Down below there were two floors of rooms that should have been spacious, but where all the space was taken up by overstuffed Victorian furniture, and where even the light the big windows should have given was defeated by a heavy shrouding of velvet curtains. Downstairs also was Authority, in the shape of her sternly religious grandparents; and in the demands that their standards made on her, she found she had to cope with yet another dimension of the gloomy wrestle with her conscience.

THOU, GOD, SEEST ME. That was the text that hung in the dining room; and it was *their* idea of God it always conjured up for her—Jehovah, God of all the battles and bloodthirst and vengeance in the Old Testament. And hadn't she always resisted the thought of believing in the mere existence of such a monster? She would *not* accept such a God, she told the text. Yet still she could always feel its stare accusing her for this heresy. And how could she be expected to solve *any* of her problems when she had to face that at every meal in this stuffy, overfurnished house?

Then there was the drawing-room text: CHRIST IS THE HEAD OF THIS HOUSE, THE UNSEEN GUEST AT EVERY MEAL, THE SILENT LISTENER TO EVERY CONVERSATION. It was becoming harder and harder to face that text, too, she realized, because every time she had to she found it giving her the guilty feeling of Christ reproaching her for having deserted the simple beliefs of her childhood years; and that, of course, just wasn't fair—not when she had already put such an effort of thinking and reading into trying to decide whether he really had been God's son or whether he had just fooled himself into thinking that was so. Yet still the guilty feeling persisted; and added to it now was the sense that Christ was quite rightly also reproaching her for her behavior that night at the Bellwood.

Granny Armstrong began to complain about her lack of appetite. "You're only picking at your dinner these days," she said eventually. "I know what *you* need, miss."

Bridie watched her rise from her seat at the dining table, and knew what to expect. "Gregory's Mixture." It was her grandmother's cure for every ill "from constipation to conscience," Bridie thought ruefully, and then, with her eye once more drawn to the text on the wall, she began yet another of her arguments with it.

"Look, God," she told it, "You know You've always had trouble with me, and I've always had trouble with You. I never could see why You had to be such a great old bully—punishing people unto the third and fourth generation and all that. But maybe that's not how You are at all. Maybe it's just the way people make You seem to be. And so I'll strike a bargain with You.

"I learned in the hospital that You *are*—that night of the operation when You became the billions of star fragments exploding in my brain. And so it seems to me, too, that You must be the something in my mind that none of my reading can explain for me, the something that makes *me* want to write. What my Dad used to call 'the little spark of the divine in man.' I accept all that now—d'You hear?—even though all the rest of the religion thing might be nonsense. But if I do that, then Your side of the bargain is that You'll have to accept me the way *I* am. You made me, after all—the rotten part of me that lashed out at poor Peter McKinley along with the decent part of me that's ashamed and sorry about that. *And* you made this part of me that simply has to think everything out for myself, that can't swallow the Bible whole the way the grandparents do. So give me a chance, will you? Just stop *accusing* me!"

"Here you are!" Her grandmother was back with the bottle of Gregory's, her plump red face made even redder by exertion and the determination to do her duty. She poured a dose from the bottle and advanced the spoon, talking all the time.

"He was an Edinburgh man, Dr. Gregory—Dr. James Gregory. Did you know that, Bridie? He lived in the time of Sir Walter Scott. 'The famous Dr. Gregory' they called him after he invented his mixture, and everybody who was anybody in those days used to swear by it. Which was quite a tribute, I can tell you, because it wasn't just great writers like Scott who were alive in his day. 'The Athens of the North,' they called Edinburgh then, just because it was so full of the great and famous in all the professions."

Bridie swallowed her dose obediently and ignored the chat even though her grandmother was a walking, talking, living history book of Edinburgh, and in normal times, she herself would have delighted in any tale that would have helped to color her own growing picture of the city's past. But nothing was normal with her now, not since she had swung up that hand with the book in it. Yet still she shrank so much from the contempt she was bound to have roused in Peter McKinley that still she dared not seek him out to say how immediately sorry she had been. And there could be no relief either, of course, in speaking to anyone else of her continuing remorse, because that would simply mean having to suffer renewed teasing about her "fella."

That was maybe the worst part of it all, she thought, to feel as she did and yet not to be able to talk to anyone about it. Not until Christmas, at least, when William and Mum would be coming together from the village to spend the school holidays in town. They had always shared secrets, herself and William. . . .

"Away with you then," her grandmother told her. "It's nearly half past one, and you know Jemima doesn't trust Bunty to manage alone when she goes off for *her* dinner."

Bridie made for the door, still cherishing the thought of William; skinny, talkative little William who could always see the funny side of things! Nothing, she told herself, was ever so bad when William was around. She quickened her step, suddenly fearful of the sharpness of Jemima's tongue if she arrived late. But Jemima had already gone for her dinner by the time she reached the shop. Bunty was alone there. And Bunty

76

was singing! Bridie heard her as she pushed open the shop door, and wondered at the sound. Then she remembered. Tonight, Friday night, was Bunty's big night for dancing. "Jiggin'," she called it, and when Bunty was "goin' to the jiggin'," she was always in high spirits.

"Oh, it's you!" Bunty had come forward at the sound of the shop bell, but when she saw Bridie, she took up her song again. *"Let the dance floor feel your leather . . ."* A couple of long glides took her across the floor of the front shop. She turned, on quick chassé steps, and slid back. *"Come on, let's get together. Let yourself go!"*

Bridie advanced, smiling at the performance, peeling off her coat as she came. Bunty seized the coat from her, tossed it aside, and planted her right arm around Bridie's waist. "Come on!" she commanded, and slid off again, taking Bridie with her. *"Step it lightly as a feather. Let yourself go!"*

The shop bell tinkled again, and the sound was followed by a guffaw of laughter. Hughie stood there, running one hand over his thatch of greasy curls, his face split by a great grin of delight.

"Jeez!" he said. "Aw jeez, you two. You look great!" He dug one hand into a pocket of his overalls, and brought it out again holding a mouth organ. "And a-one, two, three!" Skillfully he began mouthing the music of Bunty's song, and once more Bridie found herself being propelled across the floor of the front shop. But this time, lacking the surprise of the first occasion, she muffed it. This time she had two left

77

feet, and Bunty could not pull her through the rapid steps needed for the turn.

"I can't do it. Lay off, Bunty, I can't do it."

Protesting, she broke away from Bunty's hold, and immediately, Hughie was there, nonchalantly buttoning the stained old jacket he wore with his overalls, and drawling down at Bunty,

"Ya dancin'?"

His voice was nasal, an imitation of what he fondly imagined to be an American accent. Bunty giggled at the sound. But it was the smart thing to do, of course, to copy the tones of Hollywood film stars, and so she primped up her perm and drawled back at him,

"Ya askin'? Then Ah'm dancin'."

They slid off together with Hughie hoarsely crooning, Bing Crosby style, *Blue Moon, you saw me standing alone, Without a dream in my heart, Without a love of my own.* . . . Their timing, Bridie thought enviously, was wonderful. And their steps, so exactly matched, made it seem as if they were one person dancing. How did they do it? The tune was a slow one, full of pauses that lifted into a quick run of notes. How did they manage to vary their steps to take all that in? Hughie grinned as he caught the wonder in her eyes and spoke in his normal keelie voice.

" 'S easy, hen. Slow, slow, quick quick, slow—that's a' there is to it."

Bridie shook her head. "I'd like to learn. But it looks too difficult for me."

"Away!" Hughie stopped dancing, winked down at Bunty, and became American again. "Stick around, sister," he told her, and reached out a hand to Bridie. Bunty turned away, batting her eyelashes at him and saying over her shoulder, "That's okay with me, big boy." Bridie found herself being drawn close to Hughie, with his right hand clamped hard in the small of her back, and her right hand being brought up to rest within the callused palm of his left. He spoke to her, coaxingly.

"You try a quickstep wi' me, hen. It's the easiest o' the lot. And once y've done that, y'can dance anythin' at a'."

Hughie smelled. In a different way from Henry, certainly, but just as strongly. Grease, body odor, stale tobacco—they were all there in the wave of bad air coming from him. But Bunty was calling, "Step back on the left foot—on the *left* foot, Bridie," and Hughie was moving, taking her with him, and both Bunty and Hughie were singing, and Hughie's hand was so firm in the small of her back, the whole of Hughie's body was moving so close against her own, and so strongly, that there was no question of not matching her steps to his.

"Ah'll be down to git you in a taxi, honey, Y'better be ready by half past eight. . . ." Marvelous syncopation of the rhythm! *"Now, dearie, don't be late. . . ."* Hughie was grinning down at her. *"I want to be there when the band starts playin'. . . ."* And what a great guy Hughie was! Apart from the way he ponged, of course, but what was that, after all, except the smell of his slummy sort of life? No, Hughie really was a great guy. Hughie was all right. He had taught her to dance, hadn't he? And she was doing that now as if she had already spent dozens of nights at the Bellwood!

Hughie finished the dance by swinging her rapidly from foot to foot around himself in a movement he called a "Belgian birl," and then stood eyeing her with what looked like surprise and a certain cautious admiration.

"Y'r no' bad, hen. No' bad at a' for a lassie that's never cut a rug afore this. Y'd get on fine at the Bellwood."

"Away, Hughie," Bunty objected. "The Bellwood's a low dive. It's common!"

Hughie shrugged. "Good enough for me. An Ah'll tell *you* somethin', Bunty Henderson. There's some jiggin' at the Bellwood that'd put Fred Astaire in the shade."

"Aye, maybe," Bunty argued. "But you still get fights there, and the kind of chaps that go with a flask of booze in their hip pockets. She'd be better off at the Plaza, where the toffs go. Or even at the Palais. They've got bouncers at the Palais—big chaps that can break up a fight before it gets well started."

"But hey, you two," Bridie interrupted Hughie's reply to this, "the question's academic, isn't it? Because you know very well—" The grin flashing between Bunty and Hughie made her break off abruptly. What was so funny? she wondered, and understood when Hughie jeered,

"Academic! D'ya hear her, Bunty? Swallowed a dictionary, has she?"

Bunty's grin faded to a tolerant smile. "Ach well," she allowed, "it's maybe better than being pig-ignorant like you, Hughie. And she's right, of course.

It's eexy-peexy what *we* say, because her granny would never let her go to the jiggin' anyway."

Bridie was struck by a sudden thought . . . *William!* If she sneaked out to go dancing when William came to Granny's at Christmas, he could—he *would* cover up for her. Cautiously she said,

"I could get out without my granny knowing. But—" She hesitated, glancing back and forth between the other two. "I couldn't—I mean, I've nobody to go with. And I'd be scared to go on my own—not knowing what it's like, and all that."

Hughie began to laugh. "Keep y'r peepers off me, hen," he advised. "C'n ya see y'r uncle's face if he got wind y'were runnin' wi' a keelie?"

"Aye, aye, but wait a minute," Bunty told him. "*I* never needed a fella to take me to the jiggin'. And so what's to say she couldn't go with me?"

"Just that she's no' old enough," Hughie retorted. "Ah'd bash *ma* wee sister if she went jiggin' afore she was sixteen. And Ah'd bash her again if she went after her mammy said 'no.' "

Bunty broke into giggles. "You're a card, Hughie," she said. "A keelie like you, preachin' away there the same as a church elder!"

"Ach well," Hughie said awkwardly. "Ach well." Then he too, began to laugh. And all that a crestfallen Bridie could get from Bunty after that was a promise that yes, certainly, the two of them would go jiggin' sometime. But not till Bridie was old enough. Not for that winter, at least.

9

There were no further opportunities for impromptu dance lessons; or not for a while, at least.

Trade was building up towards the usual rush at Christmas, with the shop staying open later and later each day, and the orders piling up until even Hughie with his van could not cope with all of them. Bridie was pressed into service as messenger girl for the ones that had to be delivered locally. William joined her in this as soon as he arrived with their mother. And then too, as had happened on the previous year, the final barrowload of orders to be delivered late in the evening became a form of entertainment for the two of them.

Jerusalem Lane, Jordan Road, Siloam Lane, Bethlehem Place; the little back streets around Comiston had such an odd collection of names! And not the least of the entertainment was to create their own joking fantasies around these. To sing, also, all the old, tub-thumping tunes from their grandparents' Redemption Song Book as they ran with their load of holly wreaths and pot plants and mistletoe; and best of all, finally, to "cross over Jordan" and into Jerusalem Lane, where "the Promised Land" of Tonio's Café provided them with bags of piping-hot potato chips, salty, and—as William always demanded they should be—"drenched, but *drenched* in vinegar!"

It was frosty on their first night of setting out on the barrow round that year. The slap-slap of their feet on the pavement as they ran had a hollow sound. Their voices, as they called to one another through the quiet of the little back streets, sounded sharp and clear. William began counting aloud his tips from the customers, calculating how much he would have left over to buy Christmas presents after the nightly purchase of chips at Tonio's. Bridie stood indulgently by while he ran up to the doors with the orders. She had her pay, after all, small though it was, and this was William's only chance to make money. Besides which, some of the customers were so patronizing about handing out their miserable threepenny bits, and she'd be damned before she stomached that!

"I've got five shillings!" William exulted eventually. "Five whole shillings, Bridie. Isn't that terrific?"

Bridie laughed. "I've got millions," she teased, and seized William to turn his face up to the star-glittered sky. "Look, William! Someone's hit the jackpot up there, and it's pouring out silver!"

"Ach, don't be so daft!" William disengaged himself and seized one of the handles of the now-empty barrow. Bridie took hold of the other and began to sing. They were in Jerusalem Lane by then, and so the song had to be "Jerusalem the Golden." William joined in the singing, his treble voice ringing out sweetly alongside her darker tones. In Jordan Road they changed the tune to "Shall we gather at the river, the beautiful, the beautiful, the ri-iv-er . . ." and entered Tonio's Café eventually, still singing.

"You're a-merry, uh?" Tonio greeted them, and went on talking as he stood over the fryer. But Tonio's English wasn't easy to understand, partly because it was American English picked up from the time he had spent in Chicago—Tonio, for instance, still sometimes spoke of chips as "French fries"—and partly because he still used so many Italian words. As quickly as politeness allowed, they went off with the newspaper-wrapped bundles he handed them and, on the steps outside the café, sat down to open the bundles again. The smell of hot vinegar rose pungently into the night air, and William sniffed it with little moans of ecstasy breaking from him.

"Why," he asked rhetorically, "is it always Italians who make the best chips?"

"Cheeps." Bridie corrected him to Tonio's pronunciation, and added, "Because they pass the art from father to son, and Tonio is obviously a chip off the old block."

"Ouch!" William cringed from her. "Men have died for lesser crimes than making lousy puns!"

They concentrated for a while on eating; then William asked,

"All those street names around here, who d'you suppose thought them up?"

"Search me. Some Bible-punching builder, I expect." Bridie laughed suddenly. "Like the one I heard about that named streets to *his* fancy—except that he was mad keen on Wagner's operas and so he gave all his streets names like 'Wotan's Way,' and 'Valhalla.' "

"Where'd you hear that?"

"I listen to music programs on the wireless when the grandparents aren't around. On Sundays, mostly, when they're out at the Brethren's Meeting House."

"Oh ho!" William tried unsuccessfully to sound like Granda Armstrong. "So now you have to account for the sin of listening to secular music on the Sabbath!"

"That's right," Bridie agreed. "Except that I don't think it *is* a sin."

"Suppose they catch you at it."

"Suppose they do. It's not a crime either, is it, to think differently from them? Or from anyone else, for that matter of it." Bridie paused to select a large, firm chip, and to wave it like an admonitory finger under William's nose. "This isn't a Police State, you know, not like some of the other countries in Europe, where I could be beaten up, or stuck in a concentration camp, or murdered, just for *being* different."

William stared at her. "What do *you* know about all that? Police State—that sort of stuff?"

"I've been reading. Political books. Paperbacks from a shop in Forres Road that specializes in that kind of publication." *Ever since the death of Mr. Finkelstein's brother, reading, reading like mad, hunting down the kind of books that would help to piece it all together for her; learning, learning about the rise of Fascism in Europe, about Mussolini in Italy and Franco in Spain; learning, most of all, about Germany and Hitler, seeing ever more and more clearly that other things apart from the lives of Jews were being destroyed there.*

William's stare had become one of surprise. "You've changed," he said. "The way you talk—it makes you sound a lot older now."

Bridie shrugged. "Everybody has to get older."

"Have you . . ." William hesitated in his question, and then pressed on. "Have you got a boyfriend yet?"

"No. No boyfriend. But William—" She turned to look full at him. "There *is* a fellow I got mixed up with. And I've got something about him on my conscience, something really bad."

Without giving herself time then to think of how she was going to tell it, Bridie launched into the whole tale of what had happened between Peter McKinley and herself, how rotten she felt about the final part of it, and how all her remorseful feelings had somehow got mixed up with writing poetry, and God. And really, she thought when she had finished, it was wonderful the way William had let her unburden without saying a word of his own. When they talked about it afterwards, too, it was wonderful again to hear how sensible he was for his age.

After all, as he pointed out, it wasn't as if this fellow McKinley would bother to think much about anything *she* had done, not when she was really such a kid compared to him. As for who was Christ—well, Mum never pushed any of them to think as she did. And so far as the grandparents were concerned, they'd been over all that already, hadn't they?

"And," he reminded her, "you've sorted out your attitude to them."

"That's true," Bridie agreed. "But it's still awkward when they get upset over what the Brethren will say when they turn up to the Meeting House without me."

"The Brethren!" William said scornfully. "Why shouldn't you dig in your heels over that narrow-minded lot? There'll be nobody in Heaven but them-selves—that's what they believe. And so just think how awkward it's going to be for them eventually when they find out how wrong they are!"

"Oh boy!" Bridie said. "Oh, boy! What a turnup for the book *that'll* be!" She started to laugh at the picture William's words had evoked in her mind, and then controlled the laugh to add, "Okay then, I'll just have to soothe the grandparents the best way I can. Now, let's play the newspaper game, shall we?"

William immediately began smoothing out the greasy page that had wrapped his chips. "That's more like it!" he approved. "And I bet I get something before you do."

"Bet you don't! I've got a real scandal sheet here!"

Bridie was smoothing out her own share of news-paper wrapping as she answered William's challenge. It was a sheet from the kind of tabloid daily Tonio

always used for wrappers—"the gutter press," as Uncle
George always called it—and the game they were about
to play was to poke fun at its lurid contents.

Rapidly she scanned the drama-screaming headlines in front of her, the smaller print that oozed sen-
timentality as thickly as the grease that blurred it;
and in her mind as she read, a question rang faintly:
Who would ever be bothered to actually read such
rubbish? "Fat Liz, for one!" With an inward smile,
she found herself answering the question. Fat Liz had
recounted her Drama of the Tubes in exactly the style
of these same newspapers! The smile became a
chuckle uttered aloud at an item of print suddenly
leaping from the page at her.

"I said I'd beat you to it," she told William; and
then pitching her voice so that it throbbed with emotion, she quoted:

I WAS VICTIM, CLAIMS LOVE-NEST BLONDE

Interviewed today in the luxurious
apartment furnished by her financier
lover, young, blond Gloria Metcalfe (35)
sobbed out her story to me. "Yes," she
admitted through her tears, "I was 'the
other woman' in Gerald's life. But it is
a foul lie for his wife to accuse me of
wreaking havoc with her marriage. I was
simply the victim of unbridled passion
from a man who swore to me that he
was already divorced."

William checked his giggles long enough to ask, " 'Young' Gloria was a bit past her prime, wasn't she?"

"True, true. But the subeditor has to make use of any word that will help to trigger his readers' imagination; and so 'young' goes in, no matter what age he has to put in brackets alongside it. And 'blonde'—that's another trigger word. To be used, my lad, to describe anything from platinum to mousy."

William wasn't listening. William had found an item of his own. "A beauty!" he caroled, and went on to read aloud, solemnly, deepening his voice as much as he could.

CASHIERED OFFICER'S LIFE OF VICE
Handsome young Captain Neville Nicol (42) attained a dubious fame as night-club habitué, gambler, and swiller of expensive champagne from the slippers of blond chorus girls—all at the cost of his regimental funds. Grim faced after he was sentenced in Edinburgh's High Court today, he told Our Reporter,

"I have disgraced my regiment, and it is only right that I should pay for that with my freedom. But my real crime still lies in the way my life of vice has brought my gray-haired mother in tears to her grave."

Bridie was whooping with laughter even before William had reached the end of his quotation, and William himself finally went into such convulsions of mirth over it that the two of them had to hold on to one another.

"All right, you win that round," Bridie conceded once they had steadied themselves. "But let's see who gets this one."

"This one," consisted of making up their own headlines from what Bridie had called "trigger words" pieced together to make the most lurid possible suggestion of the story to follow. They turned to searching their respective newspapers, pouncing on a word here, a word there; and it was Bridie who was eventually declared the winner with a selection that read:

ROYAL VAMPIRE SCANDAL
REBEL PRIEST ACCUSES MYSTERY DOCTOR

"No doubt of it," William admitted. "There could be half a dozen stories behind that one—and all of them ghastly."

"But I bet I could make up one that would take in the lot," Bridie boasted, and as they trundled the empty barrow back to the shop, she improvised a tongue-in-cheek tale of Gothic horror that made William laugh as much as he shuddered at it.

"You should write that down," he told her. "It wasn't bad, you know. Not at all bad."

Satire . . . Well, why not? It was still another form of writing she hadn't yet attempted.

"I'll think about it," Bridie agreed. And long after William was in bed that night, she was still thinking and patiently trying to capture on paper her first exercise in the new medium.

10

Christmas Day itself, after all the rush in the shop and the nightly entertainment of the barrow round, came as an anticlimax for Bridie. And for William, too.

By the late afternoon, with dinner long past and Uncle George and the grandparents nodding in front of the drawing-room fire, they were half asleep themselves. The fire had burned low. The room was full of shadows. Bridie sat with her eyes on the pool of light where her mother was playing softly on the Bechstein grand that had been Granda Armstrong's twenty-first birthday present to her, and that had stayed behind in Comiston, of course, when she married; because how could Patrick McShane's tiny cottage accommodate such an instrument?

How had it felt, Bridie wondered, to have had to

give up anything so magnificent as the Bechstein? Had her mother resented Granda's excuse for clinging on to his own gift? Quickly she pushed the second question away from her. Her mother had never resented anything or anybody. Her mother had never shared the family obsession with trade and the money and material advantage to be won from that.

"Lively, isn't it?" William's voice came suddenly in a penetrating half whisper of disgust. Bridie turned to see him nodding towards the sleeping grandparents, and kept her own voice deliberately low when she answered:

"Be reasonable, you nit! They're old. And they don't have the kind of cash, nowadays, for the way they used to give Christmas here."

... when the whole house rang with voices, and in the downstairs rooms the sweet smell of roses was deliciously mingled with the sharp smell of tangerines, and half-recognized aunts and uncles suddenly encountered were generous, for once, in handing out silver sixpences, and Dad had sung songs that had made them all laugh ...

"You're too young to remember, of course," Bridie went on aloud, "but there were so many of us here then that the dining table had to be opened out as far as it would go. And after dinner, Granny sat with a little silver spirit lamp and a silver kettle in front of her and made tea. All the grown-ups gathered at her end of the table then, and ate little sugared cakes with their tea, while all the kids went off to play at dressing-up games. We got the run of this whole big house for that, and—"

"But if the kids all went off to play after dinner," William interrupted, "how d'you know what the grown-ups did?"

"Because I always hung around till Granda gave me one of the little cakes, of course. And sometimes, too, I used to hide under the table where it was dim and secret, like a cave, and listen to their voices rumbling away above me."

. . . Dad's voice rising a tone as he argued; Dad's voice rising almost to a shout as he told his smug in-laws, "Don't quote the Bible to me! 'To him that hath shall be given' indeed! Where's the morality of that, with half the world in a permanent state of starvation!"

The whole room, except for the small pool of light around the Bechstein, was now as dim as the one-time cave, and suddenly there was an end to the murmur of music that had filled it. The figure sitting at the piano rose, and went with hurried, uncertain steps towards the door. William turned to it, his mouth open to call out something, but Bridie caught his arm and muttered:

"Let her alone. I think she's crying."

They sat in silence, listening to the sound of their mother going upstairs with the ghost of the husband who had courted the smiling, dark-haired girl playing on her Bechstein grand . . .

"Let's go out," William said abruptly; and thankfully Bridie agreed:

"Yes, let's!"

They got their coats and ran out into the lamp-lit street, away from all the memories of Christmases past, away from the weeping woman stumbling upstairs; away, clear away from the ghost treading soundlessly beside her.

They weren't hungry, of course. They couldn't possibly be hungry, Bridie insisted, not when it was only a few hours since they'd had a large Christmas dinner. But there was William, a growing boy with hollow legs and all his usual drooling delight in the thought of hot, salty chips drenched in vinegar! Besides which, chips at Tonio's with the newspaper game to follow was a sort of ritual with them. And so that, inevitably, was how they finished up, sitting on the steps outside Tonio's with greasy newspapers spread on their knees and William chortling away over having made the first find of the evening.

"But hold on," Bridie commanded. "I think I've got something here that could be even more horribly gooey than yours." She read aloud the trigger words that had caught her eye, and then in silence let her gaze skim rapidly over the print below the bold black type that said:

> ### MUTILATED BODY ON MOOR
> A ghastly discovery was made today about a mile from the outskirts of Edinburgh's Pentlands district. Two young hill walkers, Mr. Joseph McKay (21) and Mr. James Jamieson (24) were on a hike across the Pentland Hills when they stumbled on the body of a woman. Mr.

McKay rushed to inform the police while Mr. Jamieson stood guard over the body, which was much mutilated. Graphically, afterwards, Mr. Jamieson described his ordeal to Our Reporter.

"The crows," he said, "hadn't left an eye in its head. It fair gave me a turn, I can tell you, when we found it like that."

A police surgeon who examined the body found that, very shortly before death, it had been the subject of abdominal surgery. The Health Authorities were consulted, and the body was then identified as that of a tinker woman

"Come on, Bridie." William was jogging her elbow. "Don't keep it all to yourself."

"Be quiet!" she told him sharply, and read on.

who had discharged herself from hospital in defiance of the medical staff. Other ravages to the body, which had been lying on the moor for some weeks, have been deduced by experts to be the work of foxes.

It is thought that the unfortunate woman had been trying to reach a tinker encampment reported as having earlier been on the moor about half a mile from where the body was found. Police say that foul play is not suspected, but due to the uneasy relationship between tin-

kers and the law, it is not anticipated
that anyone will come forward to claim
the body.

"Bridie?" As if from far off, Bridie heard William
speak her name like a question. She was aware of him
rising, of his voice sounding again. "Are you all right,
Bridie?"

She looked up at him. The outlines of his face seemed
blurred. She blinked, trying to clear her sight, and
fumbled out an excuse about all those chips having
been too much, on top of their dinner. William asked
anxiously,

"Are you going to be sick?"

She shook her head. "I don't think so. But it might
be better to head for home."

She rose, and began walking, with William making
encouraging noises as he trotted alongside her. She
would have to try and put a better face on this before
they got into the house, Bridie thought dully; but in
spite of all resolutions to the contrary, she found, her
mind would keep going back to the tinker woman who
had lain in the hospital bed next her own.

That squalid account on the newspaper, *that* was
what had finally happened to her. After she had fought
so fiercely, too, and then so cunningly schemed for
her escape. And yet she had wanted so little—just to
live free again, to wander under open skies as she had
always done. But all she had achieved in the end was
to die free.

I'm used to pain. Oh yes, she had been tough enough

to defy anything the doctors could do to her. But what pain, what unimaginable pain had been hers as she tried so desperately to reach her own kind again? How often on that lonely moor had she stumbled and fallen, how often forced herself to rise and labor onwards to the camp? Had she known how near she was to it when she fell for the last time? Had she known it *was* for the last time—that soon the crows would swoop down, the foxes creep out, to finish her off?

And what about the poet, Bridie McShane, in those terrible hours of the traveling woman's last journey? What about her own silly self, lying snug in bed and dreaming pretty little dreams of a Secret Princess forced to masquerade as a tinker? How could she have been so absurdly romantic, she who knew so well the true nature of the hardships the woman must have suffered! How could she have so belittled the courage that could come to terms with so harsh a reality! And faced with that suddenly empty bed, how could she have remained so blind to the tragic implications of such a fact?

Rubbish, high-flown rubbish, that was all she had succeeded in writing with her so-called verse drama. And she could see now—oh God, yes, if all her other work to date had been so feeble, she could see clearly now—how right she had been to suspect that Mr. Kendall had thought her poetry just wasn't worth criticizing! But—

"We're nearly home, Bridie," William assured her. "Can you hold on till we get there?"

She nodded, without attempting any answer in

words, her mind still hot in pursuit of that last "But—" But she wasn't going to let this last failure defeat her. She would write the tinker woman's story again, with all the stark tragedy there had really been to it. And this time it would be in prose, the spare, unvarnished sort of prose that alone could do proper justice to it. This time she would give the tinker woman a voice that would also be the voice of all her kind crying out that it wasn't such a poor achievement, after all, to have at least died free! Someday she would do that, someday *soon*. And not only because the tinker herself deserved to be given this real voice, but also because something in her own mind was insisting that she had to prove she *could* do it, or she might give up on all her writing and never want to go back to it again.

William opened the garden gate, scanning her face as he did so, and walked up the garden path telling her,

"You don't look too good yet. But you're not going to let a few chips be the finish of you, are you?"

He smiled as he spoke, a wry smile that invited her to treat the anticlimax to their evening as the kind of ironic joke they had so often shared. But this time, Bridie realized, she couldn't share with William; not until the words she would need for the tinker's story had settled in her mind and capturing them on paper would mean there was no danger of losing them again. This time she was on a road she would have to travel alone.

The thought chilled her. This worse-than-ordinary

sense of loneliness, it told her, was always going to be part of her writing, the hardest part. Yet still there seemed to be a perverse pleasure in the very realization of that—something that roused a feeling of secret defiance that had its own strange excitement for her. Guardedly she chose her answer to William's remark, but still could not keep a tremor of that excitement out of the voice that told him:

"Not on your life, William! It'll take a lot more than that to finish *me*!"

Part Two

II

Argument was in the air—"as thick as flies round a dung heap in summer," according to Bunty's phrase. Except that it wasn't summer, but the turning point of yet another year—September, with the flower shop filling up once again with the rich, the elegant blooms; and against the lush and peaceful background they made, the main word of the argument seemed all the more brutally incongruous.

WAR! Everybody, it seemed to Bridie, was talking about the threat of war against Germany. Everybody seemed to have become suddenly, sharply aware of what it really meant to have a military dictator in power there. Adolf Hitler, self-styled Führer of the German Third Reich. But nobody was laughing anymore at his grandiose title, or at the newsreel pictures that showed him with a lock of his black hair always flopping ridiculously forward over one eye when he made impassioned speeches to the huge rallies of his Nazi followers.

Sieg heil! Sieg heil! Sieg heil! There was a curious sort of silence in the cinemas now when the newsreel cameras traveled slowly over the mass of uniformed men, all shouting acclamation up to the podium decked with swastika flags and to the figure that strutted and ranted there.

Henry, of J & K Mathews, was pompous as ever when he made his contribution to the arguments about Hitler; and Henry had at last become openly a supporter of Mosley and his British Union of Fascists.

"Hitler," Henry declared, "is the kind of strong man we need in this country. After all, we've still got more than two million unemployed here, haven't we? And he's solved Germany's unemployment problem."

"Oh, *ja, ja!*" Mr. Finkelstein was sarcastic in his agreement to this. "All those not of so-called Aryan blood he drives from his country. His political enemies he puts in concentration camps. A great army he creates. Munition factories he builds. All the mothers of Germany he orders to bear sons to be his next generation of soldiers. That is good, Henry, a good solution."

It was a long time since Henry had made his tongue-in-cheek references to the Jews as "God's chosen people." Henry's secret hatred of men like Mr. Finkelstein was not nearly so secret now that he had been primed with all the usual Fascist propaganda against the Jews. He turned away from Mr. Finkelstein with the hatred plain on his face, but the other men there didn't see his expression, and Mr. Finkelstein pretended not to notice it. Granda Armstrong nodded approval of the way Henry had been put down. Uncle George said:

"And talking about this fine new army of Hitler's— it's not for show either, you know. Look at the way he's already used it to take over the Rhineland and Austria. And so what's to stop him doing the same with the part of Czechoslovakia he's claiming now?"

"Nothing," Granda Armstrong answered gloomily. "Unless the British and the French governments decide to honor the treaty that protects the Czechs. And that *will* mean war in Europe again."

"Great stuff!" Hughie exclaimed. "Ah'd fine like to have a bash at Jerry!"

Hughie had a black eye at that very moment from the kind of street fight he called a "rammy," and Bunty looked pointedly at this before she said:

"Aye, you *would*. We know your kind, Hughie."

"And if you think a war's anything like a High Street rammy," Jemima added sourly, "you'd better think again, my lad. There were millions of men killed in the last war, millions of them, including the one that left me an old maid."

Bridie felt her mind suddenly filling with the memory of a page in the encyclopedia in her childhood home. FOUR MILLION MEN WERE KILLED IN THE GREAT WORLD WAR. That had been the caption to a picture of a broad and seemingly endless column of soldiers, the young soldiers who had died in her father and her mother's war, forward-marching out of the page towards her, young ghosts of soldiers . . .

"Och aye, but—" Hughie was looking truculent enough to carry on the argument with Jemima, but he backed down before the glare she gave as she finished:

"And so it's peace *we* want. D'you hear?"

Mr. Finkelstein said suddenly, "And that, in spite of all the saber rattling, is what I think we will have. For the meantime, at least."

"With air-raid precautions already being taken in London?" Granda Armstrong asked. "The Fleet mobilized, gas masks issued, the order for compulsory military service being put through Parliament—oh, come, Finkelstein! How much nearer could we be to a state of war?"

Mr. Finkelstein shrugged. "It looks bad, I know," he admitted. "But remember this, my friend. We have at the moment a Prime Minister who believes that Hitler's appetite for power can be appeased. And already this appeaser has shown that Czechoslovakia is the sop he is willing to throw. After which, he thinks, the monster will be satisfied enough to retreat permanently to its den."

"Aw, shit!" Hughie's exclamation startled them all. "There goes ma war!" Hughie, it seemed, had not backed down after all, and he laughed as he spoke. But nobody else laughed, and it was Granda Armstrong who finally squashed him.

"Any more language like that," he said sharply, "and I'll sack you on the spot."

The misery of being forced to join that long line of

workless men standing hopelessly outside the Labor Exchange—it was the ultimate threat, and Hughie knew that! His grin became a grimace of fear. Granda Armstrong nodded in grim satisfaction at this, and then turned to tell Mr. Finkelstein,

"Well, we'll just have to wait and see. And it can't take more than a few days from now to let us know what *is* going to happen."

"Two, at the most. That is what I would say." Somberly, Mr. Finkelstein made his own estimate. But, in fact, it was only another twenty-four hours before Prime Minister Chamberlain came back from his latest conference in Germany, waving the little piece of paper that was the agreement he had made not to oppose Hitler's plans for Czechoslovakia and jubilantly declaring that it meant "peace in our time."

"Peace!" cried Henry. "I knew that Mr. Chamberlain and Hitler could agree like gentlemen!"

"Peace!" said Granda Armstrong thankfully. "And praise God for that!"

"Amen!" Uncle George responded. "Because I don't think the business could have survived another war."

"Peace!" crowed Jemima, her painted old face grinning from ear to ear. "And *this* generation of laddies won't be blown to bits!"

"Peace!" Bunty said complacently. "And I'll not be left an old maid, like Jemima."

Peace! When Mr. Finkelstein came in as usual, that day, for his bunch of roses, Bridie had a sudden flash of inspiration on what to give him. In one of the vases was a sweetly scented variety of pure white rose that had been named for the symbol of peace—a dove. She chose the six best blooms in the vase; and cheerfully, as she offered them for his approval, she volunteered:

"This kind is called 'The Dove,' Mr. Finkelstein."

She waited, smiling, for his congratulations on her choice, her heart singing, as she waited, its own small hymn of joy to the thought of peace. It was several moments before Mr. Finkelstein answered her, but finally he said:

"Ah yes, little *Nordsee* eyes. Always you choose well." Something, an emotion she could not name, passed over the big, heavy face bent towards the roses. "And tonight," he added, "when I give these to Mrs. Finkelstein, I shall say, 'Here you are, Mutti. There will be no war to claim all the young men, after all, and so I bring you roses that are also symbols of peace.' And if Mrs. Finkelstein says to me, 'But Jakob, what of all those other young men in Czechoslovakia? And the women and children, too, who must also live now under the iron heel of Hitler?' I—"

Mr. Finkelstein's hands, soft-skinned jeweler's hands, closed tightly around the stems of the roses, and with dismay, Bridie saw the bright red of blood from the thorns that had penetrated the skin. But Mr. Finkelstein had not noticed either the pain of the thorns or the blood they had drawn. Mr. Finkelstein was staring into the middle distance at some anguished vision of his own, and telling himself, almost in a whisper,

"I will not answer that question. I will not, because I cannot. I cannot bring myself to argue that all those ruined lives should be the price of *our* peace."

108

12

"We'll celebrate," Bunty announced. "You and me, Bridie, we'll make whoopee for the peace." And so the long-promised night at the jiggin' was at last about to become a reality.

Bunty chose the Palais de Danse as the scene of their whoopee, and William was let into the secret of their plans. William had just arrived to spend his October mid-term break at Granny Armstrong's; and so, Bridie explained, he could cover up for her by pretending the two of them had retired together for the evening into the attic story.

"Then later," she added, "you can slip down and leave doors unlocked for me: the one in the back garden wall and the kitchen door."

"Phew! You've got your nerve!" William was quite

ready to cooperate, yet still astounded at her daring. But the fear that Bridie herself felt was only the spice to her elation, and by the end of the tram ride that took Bunty and herself to the Palais, she was in the wildest of spirits.

The entrance to the place proved to be disappointingly small and dingy. The ladies' dressing room was also small. It was crowded, too, and the overheated atmosphere was heavy with the mingled odors of sweat and strong, cheap perfume. Bridie began to have the sinking feeling that the jiggin' might not be so glamorous as she had supposed, but Bunty was pushing a lipstick into her hand and impatiently telling her:

"Here! Your face is naked, girl. Get some of that on you."

Bridie pushed mirrorwards through the press of warm bodies. The other faces reflected by the mirror were all heavily made up, with eyes fenced in by black spikes of mascara, mouths that were Cupid's bows of scarlet. Like dolls' faces, she thought, and placed red cautiously on her own mouth as she rehearsed the other instructions Bunty had already given her.

"Stay on your feet between dances. If you park the body, fellas will think you're just waiting for your own fella, and they'll not ask you for the next dance. If you want to nab a good dancer, look out for the fellas that keep their eyes on the feet instead of on the girls' faces. They're the ones who really can dance, and you can always get one of them when it comes to a 'Ladies' Choice.' And make sure you stay right at the front of the slave market."

The slave market. That had been a puzzler, and she hadn't liked to ask Bunty to explain it; but as soon as they were through the double swing doors that led to the main body of the dance hall, she knew what it meant. All the girls there were standing in a mob right inside the swing doors. All the men were ranged around the perimeter of the floor, sizing them up. And the effect of that was just what she had always imagined a slave market to be.

The powerful odor that had filled the dressing room engulfed her again as Bunty pulled her determinedly to the front of the slave market. Faces turned towards them, marking their progress; and the faces, in spite of their doll-like uniformity of makeup, now had resentment in them. The nearer they got to the coveted front-row position where all the men could see them, the more resentment there was. Eyes flashed between the mascara spikes, scarlet mouths muttered, and from one of these eventually, came the challenge:

"Pushy, aincha?"

Bunty immediately became the swaggering gangster's moll of the cinema world. "Yeh? Wanna make somethin' of it, sister?"

The mouth subsided into sullenness. They thrust on to reach the front of the slave market, and at last Bridie was having her first real view of the dance hall. She took it all in, avidly curious, yet still with her mind tick-ticking away in that objective fashion that told her she would always remember what she was seeing.

It was big, so much bigger than she had imagined

111

that she was more than compensated for her earlier feeling of disappointment. Along the right-hand side of the floor stretched a row of small tables, with two chairs at each. Along the left was a short flight of steps leading to a shadowed balcony holding more tables and chairs. The light came from overhead, from chandeliers glittering with fragments of multicolored glass. And the dance floor had a high gleam that promised well for the result of all the snatched dancing lessons that had followed the first that Bunty and Hughie had given her!

On the low platform at the farther end of the dance floor, the bandleader raised his baton, and with trembling anticipation she heard the first, blaring notes of the next number. She looked eagerly to see who would ask her to dance, and then realized she was the only one doing so. All the other girls in the slave market had turned to chat and smile to one another as if they had no interest at all in the fellas advancing towards them. But in spite of this show of detachment, Bridie realized also, they were managing to keep an anxious eye on the advance; and from smiling at all the suddenly faked animation, she found herself on the verge of laughing aloud at it. ˙

A fair young man wearing a well-cut tweed jacket and an air of great self-assurance came to a halt in front of her. "May I ask," he inquired, "if you would care to do anything so old-fashioned as a circle waltz?"

His courtesy was so wildly at variance from the expected "Ya dancin'?" that the laugh Bridie had been holding in came bursting out of her.

"It was the first dance I ever learned," she told the tweedy young man. "In dancing class at school. And I still love doing it."

"In that case . . ." They slid off together on a floor that was still almost empty of dancers. The tweedy young man was big and loose-limbed, with a natural grace to his movements. He also laughed easily, a hearty, open laugh that seemed to indicate good nature.

"D'you come here often?" he asked. It was a stock question, to which Bunty had taught her the stock answer: "Only in the mating season." But that, Bridie decided, was altogether too pert a thing to say to this pleasant young man. Besides which it was common, and Tweedy's cultivated accent as well as his manners had placed him well above the common run.

"It's my first time," she confessed. "My first time in any dance hall, in fact."

He laughed the big, open laugh at this, and nodded in the direction of the slave market. "I rather thought you didn't belong with those predatory-looking creatures over there."

"We-e-ell." Bridie glanced uneasily over her shoulder at the girls still standing in the slave market. "Maybe not. But it's not really fair, is it, to call them predatory? I mean, when they *have* to stand there waiting to be asked, and afraid nobody will ask them—that must be really humiliating."

"Quite the philosopher, aren't you?"

Tweedy was still grinning down at her, but now there was interest beginning to temper his amusement, and honesty, when she answered him, compelled her to admit:

"No, I'm not. It was you, speaking the way you did, that made me see how those other girls must feel. But I was laughing at them myself before that."

"Let's cry *'pax'* then, shall we? I saw your smile, and it's a nice one. Besides which, you were right when you said that you had learned to circle waltz!"

It would be a pity to spoil a dance that had started so well. "All right. *Pax*," Bridie agreed, and they went on with the dance in a spirit of mutual exhilaration that had them both singing aloud before it had finished.

Tweedy—his name, she had discovered, was Eric Faulkner—thanked her politely for her company as he returned her to the slave market. But this escort, she discovered also, was an unusual courtesy. It was the thing, apparently, for a man just to walk away from his partner at the end of each dance; and the keelie who was her next partner very quickly introduced her to that custom. But he was, at least, a much-cleaned-up keelie, very proud of his suit, which was brand-new from The Fifty Shilling Tailor, and he could dance nearly as well as Hughie could.

A pimply boy not much older than herself followed on from the keelie—very nervous at first, and inclined to fall over her feet. Then came a plump, middle-aged man who was so conceited about his dancing that he just didn't seem to realize how ridiculous he looked among all the young faces there.

"Been dancing with your daddy, huh?" asked the

young sailor who took her up next and teasingly indicated the plump man before he swept her off into a quickstep that was more of a romp than a dance.

"Charming the Fleet now, I see," remarked Eric Faulkner, coming back for another circle waltz with her.

"C'mon, baby doll," a second keelie invited. "Ma pal says y'can cut a rug."

"How're you doing?" caroled a happy-looking Bunty gliding past her in the middle of the next dance. And with her glance flashing down from the giddy whirl of the multicolored lights, with the rhythm of the music pulsing ecstatically through her, and all her senses telling her that she was "in" at last on the kind of party she had so often envied, Bridie caroled blithely in reply:

"I'm doing fine! Just *fine!*"

They met again towards the end of the evening, when the near-exhaustion of having danced for over three hours had forced Bridie at last to take a seat at one of the little tables on the right-hand side of the floor. She stretched out her aching feet; and ruefully, as Bunty came to sit beside her, she said,

"My feet, oh, my feet!"

"Mine too." Bunty bent to take off her dancing slippers, and the two of them sat looking, in contented silence, around the hall.

The girls in the slave market were now fewer than before, Bridie noted, and those who had been left there had sour, frustrated looks on their faces. On impulse, she asked,

"Aren't you glad we didn't have to stand there like them?"

Bunty laughed. "Catch me being so dumb!" she said complacently. "I've got my own little tricks for letting the fellas notice me, I can tell you. And as for you—" She paused to put her slippers on again, then turned to look full at Bridie. "As for you," she repeated, "d'you know why you never once had to stand there tonight?"

Bridie gaped at her. "I never thought—I mean, I just wasn't bothering."

"That's right," Bunty agreed. "You've gone around the whole damn night looking as if you *expected* the fellas to dance with you. Grinning your head off, you were, most of the time, laughing and singing like a kid at a Sunday-school party. And not bothered in the least about nipping out to take the shine off your face, or give a quick comb to your hair. And that isn't what the fellas are used to, you see. That isn't the way the game's played at all. So you were like a—like a kind of novelty to them. And they fell for it, hook, line, and sinker, from the keelies to whatsisname—that well-dressed young gent over there."

With one hand wavering, she indicated Eric Faulkner, dancing now with a slim girl in a red dress. Bridie said automatically,

"Eric Faulkner. He's a second-year Arts student."

Bunty nodded. "Aye. So well you might know something about him, seeing the way he kept coming back

116

to ask you for another and another dance. But—"
Momentarily she interrupted herself for a quick glance
at the clock on the wall above the slave market. "The
party's nearly over now, my lass, because the next
dance will be the last waltz. And 'Who's Taking You
Home Tonight'—that's what they always play. See?"

"No. At least—" Bridie paused in confusion. "D'you
mean that, if you dance this one, you've agreed that
the fellow you've danced with will be the one to see
you home?"

"That," said Bunty grimly, "is the general idea. And
that's why the party's over for you. *I* know the score
there. But you're too dumb even to realize that all
these fellas—or most of them, at least—come here for
just one thing. And if one of them sees you home, he
expects to get it."

Bridie said in dismay, "But I thought you and I
would go home together."

"Not on your life!" Bunty laughed, and indicated
a flashily dressed young man lounging over the rail
of the balcony on the far side of the dance floor. "If I
play my cards right with that one, I can get a lot more
than a walk home out of him."

The music stopped as Bunty spoke. There was the
usual confusion of dancers milling around and then
separating, females back to the slave market, males
to drape themselves against the walls. Bunty began
a quick inspection of herself in the mirror of her powder compact.

"I'll go and get my coat," Bridie said. But curiosity
for a closer look at Bunty's flashy capture kept her

still seated. And reluctance too, she realized. Even if Bunty *had* been right, even if it *was* true that she'd had such a good time because of her own high spirits, she still didn't want the party to be over.

The lights in the hall dimmed to a gentle glow. The opening music of the last waltz came trickling out, softly played, syrupy sweet. And immediately then, all the lounging men began a beeline for the slave market. The unexpected speed and determination of their move made Bridie gape; but Bunty grinned and said:

"You see?"

Bridie smiled uncertainly in answer, and the two of them sat awaiting the approach of the flash man; but Bridie's smile froze as she realized that he was not the only one coming towards Bunty and herself. Eric Faulkner was making in the same direction; and quickly now, from the balcony, there was another figure advancing. The third figure was slim, dark-headed, and even in that dim light, even after the lapse of a year since the incident in Bellwood School, she knew immediately who he was.

To show the use of the apostrophe, one could say, "Peter McKinley's dark, Peter McKinley's handsome. . . ."

Bunty rose to the approach of her flash man. Peter McKinley and Eric Faulkner were there, each of them just a step behind him. Their voices, speaking to Bridie, cut across one another.

"May I have this last waltz?" That was Eric, casually polite as always.

118

"You owe me time, Bridie." That was Peter, curt and very decisive.

From the corner of her mouth, Bunty muttered, "Let me handle this."

"No." Shaking her head at Bunty, Bridie rose. Her legs felt weak, uncertain, but her voice was quite calm as she said, "Thank you both, but I'm not dancing anymore tonight."

"Then get your coat." The curtness of Peter's voice had not changed; but it was his words, not his tone, that made Bunty's eyes open wide in a warning glare at Bridie. She faced the glare steadily, and said in the same calm voice:

"Off you go, Bunty. I'll see you in the shop."

Eric Faulkner touched her shoulder, and as she turned to him, he said:

"If you're not dancing, perhaps I could run you home. I have my car outside."

His eyes were more on Peter than on herself as he spoke, and his self-assured manner had never been more evident. Peter answered before she could, his own glance making quick appraisal of Eric's elegant appearance.

"Fancypants," he said contemptuously, "try minding your own business while Bridie and I mind ours."

"I'll see you outside, Peter." Swiftly, on the words, Bridie turned from them both; and although she could not see Peter following as she went to get her coat, she still knew he was there, moving like a dark shadow across the floor behind her.

13

Peter was lounging against the streetlight outside the Palais, hands in pockets, hat pulled down over one eye. The hat, Bridie recognized, was the same wide-brimmed homburg he had carried when he visited her in hospital, and in spite of her apprehension at that moment, it flashed across her mind also that the rakish angle of it really suited him.

"Which way?" he asked. She gave him the address in Comiston; but instead of making for the tram stop, he said, "We'll walk there."

It was he who set the pace, his long-legged stride so rapid that she had to accept the indignity of almost running to keep up with him. But that, she supposed, was all of a piece with his curtness in the dance hall—just another sign of his determination to have it out with her over that miserable incident at the Bellwood. She waited for him to speak, thinking he was at least entitled to air his feelings about it before she gave him the further satisfaction of hearing her apologize; but it was some considerable time before he said:

"The bloke in the tweed jacket—who's he?"

"Eric Faulkner." The answer came automatically from her, even as she puzzled over the seeming irrelevance of the question.

"Friend of yours?"

"I never met him before tonight."

"But you danced a lot with him, I suppose."

Why couldn't he speak about the Bellwood business and be done with it? Impatiently, as she put the question to herself, Bridie said, "Yes, I did. Earlier on in the evening. But surely, if you were watching the floor the way they all do, that's something you don't need to be told."

"I wasn't there earlier. I'd just that minute looked in to speak to the chap who runs the electrics."

They walked in silence again until Peter said suddenly, "If I'd known! If I'd only known!"

"Known what?"

"How easy it would have been. Just keep an eye on the dance halls—that's all I would have needed to do!"

"How easy *what* would have been? And how do dance halls come into it?"

"You seem to hang around in them."

"I do not! It's the first time I've been in such a place.

And my granny would kill me if she knew about it."

"All right. You don't have to justify yourself to me."

"That wasn't the impression *I* got."

Peter veered abruptly to another line of questioning—another line of attack, as it seemed to Bridie.

"Why didn't you come back to the class at the Bellwood?"

"There was another one I wanted to take."

"Why?"

"It's more interesting. And more useful to me."

"Oh." For the length of another street, there were no more questions. Then Peter halted suddenly under a streetlamp, looked down at her, and said, "It's been quite a time now, hasn't it. A year, almost."

Here it comes at last, Bridie thought. Her eyes dropped away from his gaze as she told him, "I'm sorry. I was sorry the moment I did it, and I should have said so then, but—" With an effort, she made herself look up. "I was so ashamed I couldn't help running away. I kept on being sorry, too, but I didn't have the nerve to go down to the Bellwood and tell you so. Then I found this other class that suited me better anyway, and by that time I was telling myself that you'd have forgotten all about me and the business of the book. . . ."

Her voice trailed away into nothing. As if he hadn't even heard her attempt at explaining, Peter said:

"I didn't know where you lived. Neither did anyone else in that class. And that blasted School Secretary wouldn't give me your address. I drew a blank at the hospital, too. They said their records of you were 'con-

122

fidential.' But you told me there that you worked in a flower shop; and so I've been searching for you, this past year, in all the flower shops in Edinburgh."

"But—" With her mind spinning in dismay, Bridie groped for words. To search for her—deliberately search—for a whole year! To be angry enough for that! It was beyond belief, almost—certainly something she had never imagined could happen! "But I've tried," she managed, "I *have* tried now to tell you how sorry I was—how sorry I still am—about it all."

He searched her face curiously. "Why did you do it?"

"Could we walk again?" Bridie asked. "I'd rather speak without having to look at you."

"All right."

They walked, with Peter now setting a much slower pace, but with Bridie still keeping a distance from his side.

"I'd written some poems," she said. "It's what I do, what I want to be—a writer. I gave the poems to Mr. Kendall to criticize. That was the night I had to go to hospital. When I came back for them, he'd gone. He'd left the poems with the Secretary, but he hadn't written me a single word about them. I thought that was just callousness on his part, and I was going to tell you so when you asked me why I was so upset. Then suddenly it struck me that Kendall might have thought the poems were so bad that they just weren't worth a comment. I felt *so* humiliated then. I couldn't bear it! And it was just too horrible being held there, being made to endure that feeling and all the time knowing

I was in danger of blurting out the truth to you. My mind ran away from it into a sort of blind anger. And that's all I can tell you, except—"

For the first time since she had started her tale, Bridie looked at the figure keeping pace with her own. Its gaze was straight ahead, as hers had been till that moment; and with a sudden feeling of anger, she closed her lips on the words she had been about to speak. She would not, she told herself fiercely, she would *not* apologize again. She'd crawled enough as it was to this surly creature beside her!

"Except what?" Still without turning his head he put the question to her, and out of her anger, she answered:

"Except that I find it hard to believe *anyone* could hold spite for a whole year."

"Do you?" There was a smothered laugh in the way he said the words, and still further infuriated by this, she retorted:

"Yes, I do. And I find it hard to believe, too, that you looked in all the flower shops in Edinburgh. You'd have found me before this, if you had, because there aren't *that* many of them, after all."

"No," he acknowledged. "There aren't. Just enough, in fact, to take a year of my free time searching through them."

"Including Thomas Armstrong & Son, Cluny Road?"

His head jerked towards her. "So that's the one!"

"Yes. And you were never in there."

"I was," he said quietly. "There were two people there at the time—a woman and a man. I spoke to the woman. She called to the man, 'Do we have a Bridie McShane working here?' The man said, 'We don't give out information about employees.' "

"Wait a minute." Bridie grasped Peter's arm to bring him to a halt beside her. "What were they like, those two you saw?"

"The woman was elderly, dyed hair, a lot of makeup. The man was in his late thirties, dark hair, heavy build."

Jemima and Uncle George! And both of them, as usual, trying to run her life for her!

Peter was looking, waiting for some response to his description, his face lit by the overhead glow of a streetlamp. Irrelevantly, in the midst of her embarrassment over what she would have to tell him, Bridie noticed how blue his eyes were. She looked away from the intent blue gaze, and reluctantly said:

"The man was my uncle. He was just trying to put you off because he knows how strict my grandparents are with me. That includes not allowing me the chance of what they call 'getting mixed up with men.' And Jemima—the old woman—goes along with their ideas for me."

She had expected Peter to be annoyed at the way Uncle George had deliberately tried to fool him. But instead of that, he had begun to smile as she spoke; and resentfully she added:

"I was going to apologize for them, too. But that obviously isn't needed now."

"No. Not now." Still smiling that unexpected smile, he urged her gently forward with him. They walked in silence for the short distance that brought them to the corner of Jerusalem Lane; and there Bridie halted for the last time.

"Well . . ." She glanced up at the street sign feeling thankful it was all over at last, and yet aware, at the same time, of an odd regret over the thought of never seeing Peter McKinley again. "This," she told him, "is where I'll have to say good night."

"But we're not at Comiston yet!" Peter's eyes had followed her own glance at the street sign; and quickly she explained:

"My grandmother's house backs onto this lane. I have to slip in through a door in the garden wall, and then through another door into the kitchen. My young brother's left them both unlocked for me."

Peter laughed suddenly. "I did make a mistake, didn't I, taking it for granted you were used to dance halls!"

"It must have looked that way to you, I suppose."

"Whereas the truth is you're not really allowed to do *anything*—are you?"

Except "scribble." Not that they approved of that either, of course. But at least, they thought, it kept her out of harm's way!

Bridie said stiffly, "My grandparents mean well. But they belong to the Brethren." There was no need, she knew, to say more. Everybody, but *everybody* had laughed at some time or another over the strict ideas of the Brethren. She held out her hand, ready for a quick farewell clasp. Peter took the hand between both of his own.

"Tell them," he said, "that I mean well too. I'll call

for you on Sunday afternoon at three. At the *front* door."

"You—you'll what?" With bewilderment robbing her of the power even to withdraw her trapped hand, Bridie stood staring at him.

"Didn't you hear? I said I'd call for you."

"But you were so angry! You spent all that time searching for me *because* you were so angry!"

"I searched for you," he said, "for no other reason except that I wanted to see you again." With deft movements he swept off the rakish-looking hat and drew her forward to kiss her lightly on the lips. Still holding her, he asked, "Sunday at three?"

Breathlessly she answered, "If you want," then stepped back from him and hurried off to the door William had left open for her.

14

Peter's visit was cautiously received by the grandparents, but Bridie had at least been able to speak the truth when she was forced to explain something so extraordinary as the prospect of a young man calling on her.

"I met him at my Bellwood night class, Granny."

Any young man who attended night classes was assumed to be trying to "better" himself. And so the answer had not only let her off that particular hook, it had also been a mark in Peter's favor. But this, of course, was still only the preliminary to the cross-examination that Peter himself had eventually to face.

"And what are you studying for, young man?"

"My Higher National in electrical engineering, sir. I have a job with Sanderson's."

Another good mark for Peter! Sanderson's was a well-established firm, rock steady, highly respected.

"Bridie—" This was Granda again, staring straight at her across the width of the drawing room. "I thought you told your Granny you met Mr. McKinley at your English class?"

"But I've had to drop that class, sir." Quickly, as Bridie glanced an appeal at Peter, he fielded the question for her. "I have technical classes three evenings a week, now, at the Herriot-Watt College. And that doesn't really leave me time to pursue the English class as well."

"Ah, yes." Granda nodded, apparently quite happy with this explanation, and Bridie guessed how his mind was working. Technical studies mattered. Technical studies had to do with business. But English— well, if a man could read the stock market reports and write a good business letter, what further use was there for English?

"And when you're out of your apprenticeship," Granda pursued, "I've no doubt—eh?—that you'll be aiming for more than a job on the shop floor."

"Probably, sir. Sanderson's has various courses I could take to improve my prospects."

A textbook answer! As Bridie silently cheered it, the questioning moved to the subject of Peter's family. He was an "only," they learned then, and his father was a clerk in the Post Office. *A white-collar job!* Bridie's eyes intercepted the telegraphed message her grandparents sent to one another, read the approval in it, and rejoiced again. Peter sent her the ghost of a grin that showed that he too had noted their snobbish concern.

"And my mother," he offered, "does voluntary work for the Red Cross."

Granny Armstrong gave another smile of approval; but almost immediately afterwards, the smile grew rigid at the edges. Charity work, that was a Christian endeavor, of course, but— Sternly she asked,

"And what church do you belong to, Mr. McKinley?"

Bridie made a rapid and private deal with God. *I'll do more than admit You exist. I'll pray to you—if You let him give the kind of answer that'll please them.*

Peter said, "St. John's, Mrs. Armstrong. The one in Willowbrae, not the Princes Street St. John's."

St. John's, Princes Street, was Episcopal—halfway to Rome, in the grandparents' view. And Rome, to them, was the Scarlet Woman in the Book of Revelations. But St. John's, Willowbrae, was bleakly Protestant; and that was as near as anyone could get to their own stern brand of religion. Bridie relaxed her tense position on the edge of her chair. Granny Armstrong heaved her plump form upright, and said:

"I think we could start getting tea, Bridie, while the gentlemen continue their talk."

Granny Armstrong offered tea the way American Indians were supposed to offer a pipe of peace, Bridie told herself, and winked cheerfully, as she went through the dining room, at the text that said, THOU, GOD, SEEST ME.

130

"You managed that well," she told Peter. "Maybe too well, if you're not the paragon you made yourself out to be."

They had got away from the grandparents by then and were heading for the nearby Braid Park, each of them carrying a bag of the stale bread Granny Armstrong had insisted they should take to feed the wildfowl that made the Braid Pond their sanctuary. Peter gave an extra tilt to the rakish-looking hat he seemed to enjoy wearing, but the grin that came along with the gesture had a certain apology in it.

"Well, I certainly don't go to church every Sunday," he admitted. "Do you?"

"I never go at all."

"With those grandparents?" Peter gave a surprised backwards jerk of his head to indicate the house in Comiston. Bridie said carefully:

"My mother brought me up to have their beliefs. But now I'm trying to think things out for myself." They walked in silence for a moment or two before she added, "But however you managed to pass the test, you're respectable enough by my standards. And it has at least meant I've been allowed to go for a walk with you—although I still don't know why *you* should want that."

Peter made a pretense of leering at her and said throatily, "Just give me time, and I'll show you."

He was so obviously avoiding any real explanation that Bridie realized she had no alternative but to accept his fooling. She smiled in answer to it, a rather wry smile, and told him:

131

"Time is something you're obviously going to need—considering all I'm allowed meanwhile is to trot along with you to feed the ducks in the park."

"It's a tame enough diversion," Peter agreed. "But d'you mind?"

"Mind?" Impulsively Bridie turned towards him. "Don't you see what's really happened? You've made them begin to let go their hold on me. You've won me *some* freedom, *some* right to lead a life that isn't just work in the shop and study and trying to write. I was never further from minding anything that ever happened to me."

Peter looked taken aback by her vehemence. "D'you really mean that *is* all your life?" he asked. "You're not even allowed to go out and enjoy yourself with girl friends?"

"Oh, that!" Bridie shrugged. "That's allowed. But if you knew the kind of girls the grandparents want me to mix with, you'd see how much use it is to me. They're all so prim, so respectable—on the surface, that is. Because, you see, that's the way to get on in the world, the way to get a good, solid husband who'll supply the big house and the nice clothes and the fat banking account. Not that they talk about it like that, of course, not openly, anyway. But that's still the way they think. And they look down on me, of course, because I'm not interested in their idiotic concerns."

They were approaching the edge of the Braid Pond as she spoke and getting ready to throw their bread to the birds. Peter turned to look at her over the piece of bread he held poised.

132

"I'm not harking back to that business of the book when I say this," he told her, "but has anyone ever pointed out that you can be very aggressive?"

Bridie laughed. "Plenty of times. When my father was alive, he often used to say that—"

Abruptly she broke off there and began lobbing small pieces of bread to the mallard, the pintail, the goldeneye that had come sailing expectantly to the water's edge. Peter concentrated on feeding one of the mallards, a drake that seemed to be an exceptionally greedy bird, and it was several moments before he prompted:

"Your father used to say what?"

Curtly she answered, "That I was like him."

"Why? Because he was aggressive too?"

"Because he hated snobs as much as I do. And cruel people. He got mad at *any* kind of social injustice, in fact. And so do I."

Peter turned again to look at her, his face now vivid with curiosity. "You seem to have learned your lessons at a tender age," he said. "According to what your grandfather told me when you were out making the tea, you were only nine when your father died."

"I don't think about that. And I'd rather not talk about it."

"Was it so bad?"

"I was his favorite child. He was my god. That's how bad it was."

The mallard drake that had been watching out for Bridie's last dole of bread dipped his iridescent head towards it. She stood watching him straighten his neck to gobble it down. The mallard dived, and sud-

133

denly it was as if her mind had also dived, back into the murky depth of the past she had never wanted to speak about to anyone—and least of all to someone she hardly knew. Yet suddenly again, she found, she *was* talking to this Peter McKinley, this stranger who had somehow thrust his way into her life, talking low and quickly, telling him:

"There was another thing that made it bad. If my father could die, I could die too. That was something I hadn't realized till then. I grew terribly obsessed with the thought of Time rushing on to the moment of my own death."

"That was a morbid idea for a kid to have!"

"I know. But there were two lines of a poem that used to haunt me. *But at my back I always hear Time's wingèd chariot hurrying near.* I seemed always to have that sound in my ears."

"And now?"

"I still hear it. There won't ever be a time in my life when I don't hear it, however distant it seems to become. I know that now. But it's got a new importance too now, because—" Bridie turned eagerly to Peter; and then, at the sight of the wonder in his face, said hesitantly, "You—um—won't think I'm crazy if I tell you this, will you?"

He laughed a little. "Since you make that proviso, I probably will. But you can't leave it all hanging there now, can you?"

"I suppose not." Bridie took time to put her thoughts in order, and then said slowly, "It's like this. That feeling I got about Time—Time pursuing me—it made every experience I had seem somehow significant in ways that hadn't occurred to me before. And everything I noticed after that was so clear! For the first time in my life, I felt, I was really seeing. And though I'd always enjoyed playing around with words, that was when I knew I absolutely had to capture it all in writing."

The greedy mallard was waiting now for Peter's last bit of bread. He threw it. The creature's head dipped towards it. They stood watching it till it finally gave up hope of more and sailed away; then Peter turned to ask:

"Those poems Kendall gave back to you without saying anything about them—did you ever find out why he did that?"

Bridie shook her head. "I never saw him again. But I think I can guess at the reason. I was really only a kid at the time, and all my writing then was flowery, overromantic stuff. And Kendall was a very austere type, but he was also a very shy man—remember? I think he was probably just trying to avoid a situation that would have upset both of us."

"And is it still always poetry you write?"

"It used to be. But now I—" Bridie broke off to glance an appeal at him. "Look, I didn't mean to say any of this in the first place. Couldn't we talk about you instead and the things you're interested in?"

"Okay, if you want. But where to start, that's the problem. There're so many!" Peter frowned down at the water. "*Shoes—and ships—and sealing-wax . . . cabbages—and kings—*"

"And why the sea is boiling hot—And whether pigs have wings." Instantly, Bridie capped the quotation and smilingly accused, "You *read*!"

"Guilty!" Peter made a gesture of mock surrender. "Everything I can lay my hands on."

"Me, too. I'd rather go hungry than not have a book."

They looked at one another, laughing in sudden, mutual pleasure at the way things seemed to be turning out. Peter held out his hand in a gesture that invited her to walk with him in the woods around the pond, and said:

"Then just listen and see if you can cap *this* quotation!"

They talked their way, after that, through a long and winding discussion that compared reading tastes, that argued ideas, that had them both laughing again at times, and at other times in fierce opposition to one another.

"You have an imagination," said Peter, "that just seems to run riot!"

"And you," she retorted, "are hidebound."

"Correction. I'm conventional. I think straightforwardly about the things I've read. But you send out ideas like dragonflies darting all over the place. And catching even one of them *is* like trying to catch a dragonfly."

"I'll take that further," she told him. "Dragonflies aren't just quick on the wing. They're big. They gleam like jewels in the sun. And one day, one day perhaps for everyone to see, I'll be able to weave the right net of jeweled words that *will* capture all those big, jeweled ideas."

Peter asked wonderingly, "Do you always talk like this?"

"I don't often get the chance. But what about you? Do you always talk like you've just been talking to me?"

"No. It takes a kindred spirit to allow for that. And they're not so thick on the ground."

So there it was at last, Bridie thought, the true answer to the challenge he had evaded on the way to the park, the real reason for his seeking her out. He was lonely. As lonely, perhaps, as she herself had been, until then!

15

They parted that day on the agreement that Bridie would come to tea with Peter's parents on the following Sunday; and for the grandparents, this was the final evidence of his "respectability." With interested approval they listened to her account of the visit—the neat home, the pleasant parents—and were at last persuaded to loosen the leading reins of the Sunday afternoon arrangement in favor of the more adult one of meeting Peter in the evenings instead.

It was the High Street, then, that immediately became their stamping ground, not only because they lived at opposite sides of the town and this was a handy place to meet, but even more so because the High Street was the heart of the Old Town. And, Bridie had been delighted to discover, Peter was almost as interested in the past of the city as she was herself.

They wandered there at will on these evening occasions, talking always as they went in the way they had first talked—arguing, quoting favorite lines of poetry, making discoveries about one another—but sometimes also, now, with Bridie spinning tales out of all her reading about the romantic history of the street.

They explored all the "closes"—the narrow alleys between the tall, old buildings on either side of them. They were jostled by the keelies who had taken over so many of these buildings. But the High Street had always had as much of noisy poverty in it as courtly splendor, and they saw no reason to resent this modern version of its rough elements. They deciphered strange mottoes carved over ancient doorways, and paused always to look in wonder at the even more ancient figure of the stone unicorn rearing up from the tall stone shaft of the Market Cross. They climbed the last of the steep, cobbled slope to stand in the shadow of the Castle, perched high and grim on its great black rock at the street's western end; and from there they looked down, in wonder again, at the whole of the city spread in a glittering plain of light far beneath them.

Sometimes too, when those lights seemed to beckon, they came down from their Castle eyrie, down through Lady Stair's Close to the foot of the street called The Mound, where all the street orators of the city held forth. They mingled there with the different groups of listeners and joined in with the hecklers who shouted

139

challenges at the political speeches. They walked away from The Mound holding their own private discussions on politics; and when the weather made it impossible to walk anywhere with pleasure, they sat in steamy little High Street cafés, still talking.

Yet for all the opportunities these many occasions seemed to offer, it was still only at the tram stop where they finally said good night that Peter ever kissed her again, and then always in the same way as on that first occasion at the corner of Jerusalem Lane: sweeping off his homburg hat to let his lips touch lightly, very lightly, on her own. And secretly, Bridie realized, she was glad of this.

There were feelings in her now, she was uncomfortably aware, that she had never experienced before; and she did not know what might become of those feelings if Peter had kissed her properly—the way, for instance, she had seen it happen between Bunty and the fella who had begun to call on her in the back shop. . . .

He was the flash man Bunty had met at the Palais, this fella—her "click," as she called each successive one she picked up there. And Bunty always had a fine time with a click, which made her impatient that nothing exciting seemed to have happened to Bridie after she had clicked with Peter.

"There has to be something wrong with you," Bunty informed her. "No jiggin', no double features at the flicks, no cozy nights in the pub; never anything but talk, according to your story. You need your head looked at, my girl. Or is it your click that's got something wrong with him? Is he mean with cash?"

Peter laughed at Bridie's account of this conversation. "And what," he asked, "did you have to say to that?"

"Nothing original," Bridie admitted. "I just told her there are pleasures you can't buy with cash. Then she told me I was even crazier than she'd thought."

"She seems to believe in speaking her mind."

Bridie shrugged. "That doesn't bother me. Bunty hasn't got much of a brain, but I do at least know where I am with her, which is a lot better than having to put up with the two-faced types my grandparents think are good for me. She's generous too, although she sounds so tough. I've never yet heard her say a mean thing about anyone."

"Then what makes her speak like that about you— 'even crazier than she'd thought'?"

"Let's have some tea." Bridie turned to look toward the counter of the café that had given them shelter from the wildness of the weather that night. Limpy, the lame man who owned the café, caught the glance she sent him, and as he poured their tea, she told Peter:

"Look at it from Bunty's point of view. I spend hours and hours reading in the National Library. And not only that. I read the kind of books Bunty was overjoyed to escape from when she left school: 'dull stuff'—books about Scottish history, if you please. And what could be crazier than wasting my time like that

141

when I could be curled up with something exciting, like *True Confessions* or *Peg's Paper*?"

"Bridie . . ." Peter had begun to grin. "You're being aggressive again!"

"I'm not," Bridie protested. "I like Bunty. She's a good sort. But we just don't live in the same world, that's all." Limpy came hobbling over with their tea, and when he had turned back to his counter, she added, "And then there's my writing class. Why in God's name, Bunty wonders, do I bother with that?"

"Hmmm." Peter pretended to consider this. "Maybe that's because she thinks all writers have to be weird-looking chaps with big beards. And I don't think you'd suit a beard. Your nose isn't long enough to balance the effect."

Bridie smiled, but unwillingly, regretting now that she had ever mentioned the class. If they went on discussing it, she warned herself, she might find herself confessing some of the misgivings it had begun to hold for her. And these were matters that would be far too difficult to talk about! Quickly she reached for a way to charge the subject.

"About noses," she said. "Long ones, that is. I've been reading this marvelous book by a Frenchman who—"

"Bridie!" The emphasis in Peter's voice startled her into silence. "Bridie," he repeated, "you're dodging something, aren't you? Your class—that's something you hardly ever mention. Is that what you're dodging?"

She looked away from him towards the flurry of

142

sleet blowing across the café window. "There's no mystery, if that's what you think. It's just that I've got to a stage where I'm not too happy about it, that's all."

"It's the usual University Extension course, isn't it?"

"That's right." She smiled wryly. "Full of people like me who had to leave school at fourteen and who're all desperately trying to make up for that."

"Tell me about some of them."

"There's not much to tell."

Stubbornly Peter said, "Tell me all the same."

Bridie sighed. "Well, if you must know. I'm the youngest there except for one other, a tall, thin bloke with pale eyes and pale hair and a pale manner. He always makes a beeline for my desk when he comes in, and then—" She interrupted herself to laugh, but Peter said indignantly,

"So he makes a beeline for your desk, does he?"

Peter was jealous! Bridie laughed again as she realized this, but nervously this time. Jealousy from Peter, some secret voice was warning, could be as dangerous to those strange feelings in her as a real kiss from Peter!

"But then," she finished soothingly, "I always discover he has a pale imagination too, because he never finds anything to say to me, after all."

"So who does talk to you?"

"There's one of the women students—thirtyish, straggly hair, dresses in what she thinks is an 'artistic' way—you know, lots of floating scarves, sandals, skirts with droopy hems—she drifts over to my desk every now and then to tell me I have 'an interesting face.' Then she rambles on about something she calls 'the spiritual yearnings of youth.' She's one great fake, in fact, and the times when I don't feel sorry for her I'd like to—well, just spit in her eye!"

"Bravo!" Peter applauded. "That's what *I'd* like to do with those pretentious types!" He was laughing by then, and with the pleased sense that she was drawing a gallery of portraits for him, Bridie went on,

"Then there's this bald man, who must be fifty if he's a day. He argues all the time with the tutor. And the tutor doesn't like that."

"Why not? What's Baldy's argument all about?"

"The secret of creativity. That's his name for it, at least. He seems to think he could become a writer, just like magic happening, if only somebody like the tutor would explain this secret to him. But every time he talks like that, the tutor just loses his temper and shouts, *'You're referring to God, sir; to the workings of God through the human mind. Am I God, to explain God to you?'* "

"That's fair comment," Peter remarked. "It all sounds reasonably entertaining, too. And so why *are* you unhappy about it?"

"Why?" Bridie played for time, inwardly cursing her own vanity over this game of portrait drawing. Baldy was a fool, but Baldy's arguments were mixed up with her own problem. And wasn't she an even bigger fool not to have realized where any talk of him would lead?

144

Peter's voice broke into her thoughts. "You haven't got anyone to tell except me, have you? And you do want to tell it."

She looked at him, aware at last of the truth in her own mind. It would be hard to talk about, certainly. But it was becoming even harder now to keep it to herself. She began speaking, slowly, arranging her thoughts as she went along.

"It's mostly, I think, because I have the feeling that the tutor rather despises us all. Not because we're an Extension class, you understand. He's not snobbish about that. My feeling is that he thinks all of us— underneath, at least—are just like the bald man: aspiring writers looking for a secret that doesn't exist, except inside ourselves. If any of us ever *are* going to be real writers, that is. And because he thinks that of us, he's sure we'll never be anything of the kind."

"Wait a minute!" Peter was looking very serious now. "That's rather a harsh judgment on the man. And if you're being hard on him, doesn't that mean you're making things more difficult for yourself?"

"Maybe. I can't be sure." Bridie looked away from Peter to hide the tears of self-pity she could feel pricking her eyes. "When I was fourteen, you see, and on my way to Edinburgh and my first job, I thought that all I needed to be a writer was a candle in my room and a little time to myself. And I'm unsure of myself now, I suppose, because it just hasn't turned out like that."

"But your poetry—"

"My poetry's part of the trouble. I want to go on

with it, of course. Yet now I find myself wanting to write in other ways, too. But which one would be best for me? *That's* what I can't decide. And feeling the way I do about the tutor, how could I ask him about it?"

"Listen!" Peter leaned forward to fix Bridie's gaze with his own. "What d'you love best—apart from your writing, that is."

"I thought you knew that! My study in the National Library, of course. Reading about this city, this country: what made it, what shaped the people in it—the ordinary ones among them, the poor people who got trampled on by the rush of great events unless—" In a flash of memory from her recent reading, she finished, "—unless they were lucky enough to have someone like Bowed Joseph among them!"

"And who," Peter asked patiently, "was Bowed Joseph?"

"Ah, well!" Bridie smiled at him with the sense of anticipation that always came to her when she had a story to tell. "That's quite a curious tale! Bowed Joseph was a cobbler, a humble mender of shoes in this city, a hundred and fifty years ago. They called him Bowed Joseph because he was a hunchback, and he wasn't so humble either! He was a very silent man, but he used to think a lot; and when he had thought sufficiently about any injustice the poor had suffered, he used to act. He'd sally out into the High Street, beating a drum he kept for that very purpose. And he'd beat and beat that drum till he'd gathered a huge crowd of people around him, all of them armed with the tools of their various trades—because all of them, of course, knew exactly what Bowed Joseph meant to do next! They were his army, you see, and marching at the head of that army, he could force the rich merchants of Edinburgh's Town Council to make amends for any wrongs they had done to these poor people— like cornering the market in grain, for instance, and then keeping the price artificially high. What's more, he never got a penny for himself out of all these crusades. But one thing he did get, and kept for all of his life, too. That was the absolute loyalty of his ragged army. And so, till the end of his days, also, that hunchback cobbler was the real ruler of this city."

Bridie sat back, smiling, looking for the effect of her tale on Peter, and felt it almost like a blow when he said:

"Bridie, you are the prize idiot of all time!"

She glared, so outraged that she only half heard him continuing, "You love to cram your mind with all that historical detail. And you're a natural-born storyteller. Yet you still haven't the sense to see the conclusion you should draw. You're still blind to the one thing that would give you most *joy* to write." He rose abruptly, cramming on his hat, sweeping her scarf and gloves off the chair beside him. "Come on," he ordered, "we're going to walk."

"But the weather—"

"Never mind the weather. It's suddenly become urgent to visit an old friend of mine."

Peter had her out of the café, still protesting, and straight into the cold blast of wind sweeping the High

147

Street. His hand relentless in its grip on her arm, he hurried her across the street to Lady Stair's Close, and through the close to reach the downward slope of The Mound. The wind hit them sideways on then, and with her face buried deep in her scarf, Bridie decided that she'd had enough of Peter for the night, and of this nonsense about walking, too. She would get the first tram home from Princes Street, she vowed; but once again, when they'd reached the corner The Mound made with Princes Street, Peter would not listen to her.

"You have to meet my friend," he said stubbornly, and urged her forward to the almost-deserted south side of the street, where the public gardens lay. For another couple of minutes after that, he hurried her along; then suddenly he stopped and turned her to face the railings that bounded the gardens.

"And here," he announced, "here *is* my friend!"

"Where?" Bridie peered through the railings to the graveled path and the neat flower beds that lay beyond. Her gaze traveled upwards, tracing the two-hundred-foot spire of the Scott Monument rising from the grass immediately inside the railings. In the arched portico at the spire's base was a seated figure—a white marble sculpture of the man the monument commemorated; and with her gaze coming back to the sculpted figure, she exclaimed,

"Oh, I *see!*"

"I wonder if you do see," Peter said. "How many of Scott's books have you read, Bridie?"

"Oh, quite a few. My Granny's always going on about

him—'Sir Walter Scott, the greatest writer our country has ever produced!' She has all of his books." Like the beginning of a drumroll, titles began to sound in her mind—*Ivanhoe, Redgauntlet, The Talisman* . . . And staring again at the white glimmer of the seated figure, she added dreamily, "Wonderful stuff they are, too!"

"Exactly! Because he wasn't only a great writer. He was also a great storyteller. The best! What's more, friend Wattie dug around in history the way you do, and it was out of what he found there that he created all those marvelous tales. It was what he enjoyed doing. It was his gift, the same gift *you* have, you idiot. And if you can't see—"

"Oh, don't be so daft, Peter!" Bridie began to laugh a little on her interruption. "I *would* like to write that sort of stuff, of course; and maybe it is the thing I'd do best. But spinning a small tale like Bowed Joseph is a lot different from writing a whole book. I couldn't do that!"

"Maybe not," Peter agreed. "But just think of the fun you'd have trying!"

Bridie thought, with excitement rising swiftly in her at the idea. "I wish," she said, "that we'd come before they locked the gardens for the night. We could have paid a closer visit then."

"We still can." Peter took a swift look around to make sure they were still alone on that side of the street, then clasped his hands in front of him to make a step. "Come on," he told her. "Over you go!"

149

Gingerly stepping, Bridie placed a foot on the hands held low to receive it. She grasped the uprights of the iron railings, stretching as far up as she could reach; and with Peter pushing her higher and higher yet, she got her other foot onto the horizontal linking the uprights. One final upward heave then, and she had jumped clear of the fence to land on its farther side.

Peter had scrambled up and over by the time she was on her feet again; and smothering down the laughter that seized them both at that point, they walked towards the monument.

The seated figure was awesome, seen at close quarters, larger than life-size, white marble robes frozen majestically in flow around it, and lying at its feet a great hound sculpted in the same stone. Yet there was something touching too, Bridie thought, in the forever-stillness of the hands enfolding the closed book that rested on the figure's knee; a sadness in the pose of those hands seemed also to mark that a great flow of story had halted when this man died. Quietly, as she and Peter stood looking, she said:

"I like your friend."

"I knew you would," Peter told her. "Wattie always was a popular chap!" They both laughed again at this irreverence; than Peter said, "But hush now, because this, you know, could be a historic moment." He moved a few steps from her, leaving her to guess at his intention, then took off his hat and addressed the seated figure,

"Honored sir! May I present to you the latest in your long line of heritors, Miss Bridie McShane. And may I assure you, Sir Walter, that she will be a worthy upholder of the tradition you have created."

Grandly he flourished the hat, and swept her a bow. With equal flourish, he bowed to the seated figure and then backed away so that she stood alone before it.

"What can I say?" she thought. "What can I say to him?" But it was not the long-dead writer who was in her mind. It was Peter. And whether the tears she could feel stinging her eyes were tears of laughter at his fooling or tears of gratitude for his effort, she could not tell. But at least they were not the tears of self-pity she had felt in the café; and when she turned to Peter again, she did not mind his seeing them.

16

Christmas, that year, was a different affair from those in previous years—beginning with Bridie's discovery that she was to work late in the shop instead of going out as usual on the barrow round.

"William's big enough this year to handle that by himself," Uncle George said. "And the way things are now, he'll just have to."

"But why?"

"Because we need you here, that's why. Because Bunty's doctor has just told her she's got to take it easy for a while."

"Oh!" Bridie was surprised, and a little shocked. Bunty had always *looked* so healthy! "That's a shame." Involuntarily the expression of sympathy followed on her exclamation, but Jemima and Uncle George ex-

152

changed glances at this, and Jemima said acidly:

"You can save your breath, Bridie. Bunty's made her bed, and now she's just got to lie in it."

That was all the explanation either of them would give, and so there was nothing for it but to tackle Bunty herself.

"H'mph!" It was a very pale and defiant-looking Bunty who received Bridie's questions, a Bunty who gave an impatient toss of peroxide-blond curls before she answered:

"Oh, be your age, girl! I'm in the club, that's what's wrong with me."

"In the club?" Bridie had never heard the phrase before; and even more impatiently, Bunty offered some variations on it:

"I've got a bun in the oven, you dummy. I'm away with it. Expecting."

The meaning penetrated then with a vengeance. Bridie stared in dismay. "Oh, Bunty, I'm sorry. I really am sorry. Will the father—" She checked herself, wishing she had never ventured on the question. But Bunty had no qualms over voicing it for her:

"Will he marry me? You bet your sweet life he will, or he knows the sherickin' he'll get. *And* he knows the paternity suit I'll slap on him if the sherickin' doesn't bring him to heel."

The words were hardly out of her mouth before her white face went even whiter; and suddenly she was sitting at the table in the back shop, head bent into her hands, weeping, and saying brokenly:

"But that's not the way I wanted things to be, Bridie. I wanted to marry a decent lad. And he's a work-shy, a layabout. Never does anything but bet on the dogs and drink his winnings. Yet my bairn's got to have a name, hasn't it? And even a flash man's better'n nothing when it comes to that. . . ."

The flash man at the Palais—the one who had always made such a show of his lingering kisses! Bunty's sobs were continuing. She was running her hands through her hair, disordering all the carefully arranged curls. Poor Bunty! Poor, generous-hearted, lively little Bunty! Bridie hovered over her, longing to hug her, to lay a hand on the tousled head—anything to show her sympathy; and at the same time inwardly cursing the stone-faced attitude of Uncle George, the righteous contempt of Jemima.

But would Bunty really welcome sympathy from her—the dummy, the crazy kid? Would Bunty really understand how truly sorry she was to see all that earthy cheerfulness laid so low? Bunty herself resolved the dilemma, smearing away her tears with one hand, raising the other to clutch the one Bridie held hovering near her.

"I'll manage," she said. "Thanks, kid, but it's okay. I'll manage." She rose, glanced in the mirror, and gave a hard little laugh at the appearance it showed. "It seems," she added, "that women have to. It's what you might call their lot in life."

But not in mine! Passionately, as she watched Bunty repair the ravages of her tears, Bridie made the vow to herself. She would keep *her* life in *her* hands. It would be, as she had always meant it to be, a writer's

154

life. And never, ever, would she sacrifice that, either in or outside of marriage, to any man!

"You'll meet all the rest of my family soon," Bridie told Peter—because this was the other thing that would make Christmas a different affair that year. For once, it was not only William and her mother who would be there with the grandparents and herself. For once, the Others were going to be able to travel from the jobs that had scattered them all as a family. And it was strange, Bridie thought, how the mere prospect of seeing her sisters again made her realize how much she had missed them!

William and her mother appeared as usual at the beginning of the school holidays; and even more eagerly than she had awaited them, she found herself waiting then for the arrival of the Others. They came singly; but by the evening of the day before Christmas Eve, they were all there: Nell, as energetic as any of the dogs she worked with; Aileen with her pink, unmadeup nurse's face; Moira with the sophisticated air that always sat on her as easily as the clothes of her own, very professional, making.

The house woke up, became suddenly alive again, as suddenly, it seemed, as if someone had pressed a button that took them all back years in their lives. Feet pounded up and down stairs. The attic floor was busy, and loud with voices. The downstairs rooms were once again magically full of the mingled tangerine and roses smell.

In the downstairs rooms too, Granny Armstrong

and Mum went about humming like a couple of queen bees contentedly sharing a hive. Granda's big bass voice could be heard in snatches of carols. There was much mysterious rustling of paper, laughing, and shouting back and forth from room to room. And teasing, of course. The Others had always been great at teasing; and because of Peter, that year, Bridie became their first target.

"How did she manage it?" With voices rising in mock amazement, they turned to one another after they had encountered Peter sharing a cup of tea with her and William in the kitchen. "How did little Miss Head-in-the-Clouds ever manage to get herself a real, live boyfriend?"

"Don't tell them," William counseled. William, as the only boy among so many girls, had suffered more than his share of teasing from the Others; and William, of course, had always been ready to spring to her defense. But that, Bridie thought, was all in the past, and she was quite able now to take care of herself.

"I met him at night school," she said. "And then—" She paused, aware that she had a bombshell to deliver, and grinning at the thought of it. "And then he walked me home from the Palais."

"From the *Palais*!" All three of the Others were now genuinely amazed. "You went *dancing*? Oh, you never. You never did! You're making it up, aren't you?"

"No, she's not," William insisted. "She sneaked out one night to the Palais. And I helped her."

"Oh, this is rich!" Nell gave an upward jerk of the

156

head to indicate the attics. "Come on! Upstairs, and tell us all about it!"

They hurried upstairs in a body, giggling and pushing at one another as they went; and in the safety of the attic story, Bridie told them of the dancing lessons with Hughie and Bunty, the stolen night at the jiggin', and the walk home with Peter. But not of the business with the book at Bellwood School. That, she knew, was one point where she could not survive teasing from the Others. Besides which, some instinct warned, it was something that Peter himself would look on as private.

"Are you telling the truth?" Aileen demanded, "There were actually two of them fighting to take you home?"

Aileen's pink face had its most severe look. She would make a good hospital matron one day, Bridie thought, and confidently corrected:

"Not 'fighting.' Arguing—the Eric Faulkner bloke and Peter."

Moira said, "And Peter had searched for you for a whole year!" She rolled her eyes, contorted her elegant features into a clown's grimace, and added soulfully, "It must be LUV, girls. It must be ell u vee!"

Bridie's cry of "Rubbish!" went unheeded while William and the Others shouted with laughter. Then Bridie herself laughed, with only the faintest pang of disloyalty to Peter. It was the effect Moira had always had on them all, she excused herself, and how could she possibly resist the chance to enjoy it again? Once the laughter had subsided, however, William took off on his own affairs. William, it seemed, had the sense to realize they would all now embark on purely girls' gossip; and with him out of the way, the Others settled down to the serious business of finding out about Peter.

"Parents," Aileen said briskly. "Have you met his parents?"

Bridie nodded. "Yes, and we got on very well together."

"What's the mother like?" Nell wanted to know. And remembering the blue eyes, as blue as Peter's, Bridie said:

"Oh, pretty. And so small! She's like a little Dresden doll, she's so small and pretty."

"Petite," Moira remarked. "That's how we'd describe her in our trade."

Aileen pursued, "And the father?"

"He talks a lot. Reads serious stuff, like politics and economics. Nothing remarkable to look at, but he's interesting."

"In that case," Moira decided, "Peter must take after his mother. Because he certainly is handsome. Romantic-looking too!" She glanced admiringly as she spoke at her own sleek and striking self reflected in the dressing-table mirror, a gesture that set them all laughing again, till Nell looked at Bridie and said:

"But don't be too sure that's all there is to him."

"Oh, it's not!" Bridie's agreement was instant. "Peter's very well-read. He's interesting in all sorts of ways."

"That," Nell answered, "was not what I meant."

"Oh?" Bridie looked blankly at her. "Then what *are* you talking about?"

Nell made a show of picking away some of the dog hairs that invariably clung to everything she wore; and when she spoke again it was in an even more deliberate way. "When you've trained dogs for years, as I have," she said, "you develop some of the sixth sense that *they* have about people. And what my sixth sense tells me is that there's a very hard streak in the nature of that romantic-looking young man."

Bridie had a sudden uneasy memory of the way Peter had dominated the dispute with Eric Faulkner at the Palais. She shook off the feeling of uneasiness, and said defensively:

"Well? Suppose there is. What difference will that make to me? He's only a friend, after all. Just someone to talk to."

The Others exchanged glances, all of them smiling a little; then Moira asked:

"What have his other girls been like, Bridie? Nobody could call you a type, after all, and yet men do tend to be attracted always to a particular type."

Other girls . . . Somehow she had never thought of Peter having gone out with other girls! Bridie became aware that she was looking at Moira with her surprise openly showing. Moira grinned at the expression.

"Oh, come on!" she urged. "Where d'you think he spent his time before he met you? In a monastery?"

Damn Moira and the way she could trip people into making fools of themselves! With her face suddenly an embarrassed red, Bridie snapped:

"I don't think that's funny!"

Moira only shrugged at this, but Nell said scornfully, "Oh, be your age, girl! Talking's all very well, but you can't always go round in such a dream."

Bridie's embarrassment became charged with annoyance. *Be your age!* It was only days since Bunty had thrown the same challenge at her!

"All right," she retorted. "So I *am* dreamy. But I'm not a fool, you know. Not such a complete fool as you think, anyway."

"Then you must know very well," Nell pointed out, "that your Peter won't always be content with just talk. And so tell me this, Bridie. When that day does come, how long d'you think it'll be before you have to reckon with that hard streak in his nature?"

17

Bridie found Nell's question lingering uneasily in her mind, hovering there like a signal that warned of some rock of change lying ahead.

Strenuously she tried to ignore the signal. Nell had been wrong. There couldn't be change in a friendship where two people had so much in common as Peter and herself. Stubbornly, after the Others had gone, she rehearsed the accusations she had thrown out to counter the question. Nell had always loved to dramatize things. Nell was always bossy, always setting herself up as a know-all. . . .

"You're quiet tonight," Peter challenged her.

They were walking up the High Street in the direction of Limpy's Café, opposite Lady Stair's Close. It was several nights since they had met, what with the Others having so recently departed; and so by all accepted practice, Bridie realized, she should have been chattering freely.

"I was thinking," she excused herself; and shaking away the memory of Nell, she grasped at the first topic that came into her head. William, with his school holidays not yet finished and his country boy's determination to make the most of his last few days in town; Peter had always enjoyed hearing about William. She began talking about William's plans, and then became suddenly aware of Peter turning to her with an unaccountable look of alarm.

"Wait a minute!" He spoke rapidly, interrupting her flow of talk. "Did I hear you properly just now—about William going to The Mound?"

"Yes, of course. I said he was going to hear the speakers there. He's never done that before, you see, and a country kid like him, it's—"

"When?" Quickly again, Peter interrupted. "When, *when*?"

"Tonight, he told me. Just like I told you a moment ago."

"That's what I thought you said." Peter drew a deep breath, then let it out explosively on a series of questions. "Don't you read the papers? Don't you know what's happening there tonight? Don't any of that smug family of yours know what's going on around them?"

He had grabbed her by the arm in the middle of the questions and was rushing her up the street towards Limpy's. Bridie cried out in protest against his

162

actions, in bewilderment over the meaning of his questions, but with the door of the café beginning to loom up on them, his continuing stream of words began to make sense to her.

The Fascists—Henry's admired Blackshirt pals— were holding a rally at The Mound that night. It had been announced in the newspapers, and so *someone* in her family should have seen it. Someone should have had the sense to keep William away from The Mound with that going on. Because it would mean trouble there. A Fascist rally always meant trouble— a riot, as often as not, like the one that had happened the last time, when a man had got his eye poked out. And William, at that very moment, could be caught up in another such riot.

Peter had the café door open and was pulling her to a table, telling her to wait there while he went down to The Mound to see if he could find William among the crowd.

"Get yourself a cup of tea," he added, "and I'll be back with him as quick as I can."

"No!" Bridie clung to his arm. "He's *my* brother, and I'm coming with you."

"You are not!" Peter broke her hold and pushed her into a chair. The little lame owner of the café turned to stare at the scene, but Peter paid no attention to the stare. "Don't you understand?" he went on. "I'm going because William could get hurt. That means you could get hurt too. And so you've just got to stay here."

Limpy hobbled to his counter to add sudden support to this. "That's right, hen. I've been mixed up with a Fascist mob at The Mound. And it's ugly!"

"You see?" Peter threw a grateful look at the lame man, then turned to the door. Over his shoulder as he went out, he called, "And don't budge till I get back!"

The door clanged shut. Limpy came over to Bridie's table, put a cup of tea on it, and asked sympathetically:

"Your brother, you said?"

"My kid brother. He's only thirteen."

Limpy gave a cluck of disapproval. "Somebody's daft to let a bairn of that age mix wi' them bully-boys!"

Bridie leaned her head in her hands and stared at the brown swirl of tea in her cup. The grandparents were old. Mum had no idea of what went on in Edinburgh street life nowadays. The Others had gone. But even if all that hadn't been so, she herself was still the somebody who should have checked before William was allowed to roam at night on his own. They'd always been so close, the two of them, and she always had looked out for him before.

The café was overheated. She shrugged off her coat, rose to hang it up, and took a glance around that showed her only three people there, apart from herself.

"Not much doing tonight," Limpy offered.

But it wouldn't be like that down at The Mound! Bridie glanced at the clock behind the counter. Peter had been gone more than half an hour. If he wasn't back by nine o'clock with William, she decided, she would go out herself to search for him. And to hell with anything Peter had said!

Two of the other customers went out. The third one departed, and Limpy began to chat to her. It was three years before that, he said, that he'd tangled with the Blackshirts, in the days when he'd been a member of the Communist Party, and the Commies, of course, had sworn to stop that bastard, Mosley, and his Blackshirts from ever holding a meeting. But all that had turned out to be too rough for a peaceable chap like him, because that was when he'd got his leg broken. And not even for the CP was he going to get another broken leg. . . .

On and on went his voice, with Bridie growing more and more sickened by the monologue. Communists, Fascists, dictators of the left, dictators of the right—what was there to choose between them!

"You Commies," she said bitterly, "you're as bad as the Fascists. You're both out for mob law, aren't you? And if my brother gets hurt—" With another glance at the clock she began pushing aside her untasted cup of tea; but the gesture was only half completed when the café door swung open suddenly to let in the figure of a man—a keelie type with a great gash on one cheek sending runnels of fresh blood down his face.

"Y'd better bolt up, pal." The keelie made straight for Limpy, and began hoarsely whispering. "There's Blackshirts on the way, and they've got long memories for chaps like you!"

Limpy's startled face went white. "But I've left the

165

CP now," he protested. "It's nearly three years since I left."

The keelie shrugged, with one hand going up to finger the gash on his cheek. "Please yourself. But Ah'm tellin' you, there's been a right rammy wi' Commies and Blackshirts mixin' it, and now the Blackshirts have got the Commies on the run. They're headed up this way, an' the Fascists are out to pay off old scores. As many o' them as they can."

Limpy made no further argument. As fast as he could he began hobbling towards the door. But Bridie had no limp to hamper her movements, and seconds before he could shoot the bolts that would shut her off from any chance of finding William, she had brushed past him.

"Hey you!" Limpy's voice shouting to her, Limpy yelling to her not to be so daft, that she would get herself killed, was a blur of sound behind her as she blundered, coatless, into the High Street and straight into a huddle of figures blocking the pavement outside the café.

"Let me through!" Shouting, she fought a passage through the figures and on to the roadway. Noise assailed her, honking of horns from a line of traffic slowed to an inch-by-inch crawl, the clanging of a firebell, voices yelling, feet running. Desperately she tried to thread a way through the line of stalled traffic, and found herself being pushed, buffeted, flung aside, by equally desperate figures thrusting in the opposite direction. Another sound was added to the din—a unison chant of men's voices, the Blackshirts roaring their leader's name like an invocation to battle:

"Mos*ley*! Mos*ley*! Mos*ley*!"

Bridie reached the opposite side of the road in time to be aware of them breaking, like a black boil bursting, out of the narrow opening into Lady Stair's Close. A man ran towards her. He was crouching, with both hands held to his head, and the Blackshirts were after him. She stood there in a paralysis of fear that made it all seem to happen with the deliberation of a slow-motion film—the crouching man's movements as feeble and disconnected as those of a broken clockwork toy, the black-clad pursuers spreading out to head him off in a maneuver as leisurely as the prolonged opening of some enormous fan.

An arm moved past her face, a black-sleeved arm with brass knuckledusters on the hand at the end of it, and this movement of the arm was also part of the dreamlike slowness. The crouching man collapsed at her feet. There was blood spattered on his head. The brass-knuckled fist swung down to the bleeding head. She screamed, and heard the sound as if it had been the voice of some other person screaming. But in the moment of her screaming, she was seized from behind in a grip so powerful that it lifted her bodily from her petrified stance and jerked her immediately clear of the melée around the fallen man.

The gripping hands set her back on her feet and roughly hurried her into the dimness of a close. She felt her shoulder scraping along the wall of the opening and heard at last the voice that belonged to the rescuing hands—a hoarse, keelie voice that demanded:

"What the hell were *you* doin' in that mob?"

She twisted around towards the sound of it—the familiar sound—and saw the battered features, the mop of curly hair, that belonged to Hughie.

"Oh, Hughie!" In weeping relief she fell against him, and buried her face in his sour-smelling jacket.

"Hey, hey! Y'r a' right. Y'r a' right, hen."

Hughie gripped her shoulders, making her stand straight against the interior wall of the close. "Lucky Ah was there, eh? Lucky that Hughie never misses the chance o' a rammy. But y'r a' right, now."

There were still shouts and yells coming from the street beyond the close, but with Hughie to soothe her, there was not the same terror in their sound. Hughie was listening, his head cocked towards the noise.

"They're searchin'," he said. "Searchin' for Commies to bash."

The entrance to the close was suddenly darkened by the figures of men. In the same moment, Hughie pushed her hard against the wall, bent his face to hers, and began to kiss her. She yielded to the kiss, from astonishment at first, and then with realization of the tactics behind it. The narrow openings of the closes were the favored courting places for High Street keelies and their girls. And if those dark figures in the entrance were indeed some of the Blackshirt thugs, the most effective way to be rid of them was to pretend

168

that Hughie and she were just another of those harmless courting couples.

Hughie's face twisted sideways against her own. "They're off!" He whispered the words, then lifted his head and said aloud, "It's okay, hen. They're away."

He stood with head turned towards the entrance, listening as he had before. Bridie stayed motionless, her back to the wall of the close, and listened with him. The street was much quieter now, she realized. The sound from it, in fact, had died back to almost its normal level. Hughie looked down at her. He was grinning, as if at some private joke, and the sight of his grin sent an odd leap of excitement through her. As if he had guessed at the reason for that odd feeling, Hughie said softly:

"That kiss, hen. It was no' bad, eh? No' bad at a'."

He bent his head to her. His arms came round her, drawing her body close to his own. His lips touched hers—*and hers were suddenly as hot and moist as his were, and she could feel the tip of his tongue between her lips, and her body, her whole body was in tumult, the feelings buried deep in her were all free now, wildly free. . . .*

Hughie lifted his head from the kiss, grinned down at her, and said in a surprised voice:

"You're a deep one, eh? Ah never knew y'were *that* kind o' girl!"

Bunty's kind . . . As the words flashed across Bridie's mind, memory flooded back into it also: the memory that had been chased from it by the impact of that kiss. William! And Peter, too—both of them maybe lying at that very moment in some gutter with heads bloodied like that of the man struck down in the High Street.

"Let me go!" With shame lending savagery to her actions, she began struggling out of Hughie's arms. But Hughie was a different proposition from creepy Henry. Hughie simply gripped both of her hands in his own hard ones, and said teasingly:

"Aw, c'mon, Bridie. A bit more, eh? A wee bit more."

"No!" She struggled to wrench her hands free. "You've got to let me go, Hughie. I wouldn't have been here like a—" She stopped short, choking on the words in her mind. *—like a High Street slut "up a close" with her fella.*

"What's wrong?" Hughie was staring at her, surprised by the sudden limpness of her hands in his. With an effort to regain control of her voice, she told him:

"William. He was at The Mound. Peter went looking for him. I was looking for him, too, when you pulled me out of the mob."

"That's different!" Hughie dropped her hands. "Why did you no' tell me that before, y' daft wee gomeril!"

He started towards the entrance of the close, Bridie following at a run. Outside, the street seemed to be no different from usual, and with a swift glance right and left, Hughie told her:

"Ah'll go up the way, where the mob went. You work y'r way back to The Mound. Ah'll meet y' there. Right?"

"Right!" Bridie turned to begin working her way

170

down the street, and had gone a mere ten yards when she saw them, Peter and William both, coming towards her. She broke into a run, shouting and waving to them, not heeding the surprised faces that passersby turned to her, and swept down on them to clutch William to her, and cry:

"You're safe! Oh, William, you're safe!"

"Och, come on, Bridie!" William fended her off, startled by her display and embarrassed by the amused attention it was attracting. "You're making a fool of me!"

Peter began to laugh. She saw that he was pale, and realized that the laugh was no more than reaction to the strain he had been through.

"Don't be so hard on her," he told William. "She wasn't to know you'd managed to steer clear of the mob before I found you. And besides"—he paused to laugh again, a more normal sound this time—"she's quite well-behaved, as a rule." He threw a teasing glance at her. "Aren't you, old girl?"

Herself and Hughie standing in that close . . . Bridie looked away from Peter's glance. Aloud, she said, "Don't ask me, Peter. I don't really know what I'm capable of." And silently to herself she added, *But, by God, I'm beginning to find out!*

171

18

There could be no going back to things as they had been before the night of the riot, Bridie realized. Change was happening, in spite of herself. And even as this was borne in on her, she found herself being caught up in other forms of change.

She was promoted to Second Hand when Bunty left the shop to marry her flash man. That was only two weeks after the riot, in the middle of January that year; and with a new apprentice to do all the donkey work of the shop then, she began to feel what it was like to have a little authority and a real chance to use the skills she had learned. With the increased wage Uncle George was forced to pay her then too, she was able also at last to dress decently, instead of always having to be content with hand-me-downs from the Others.

The thrill of being able to walk into a shop and buy exactly the dress she wanted went to her head a little. She began to use makeup, very discreetly, of course, so as not to offend her grandparents. But even a little powder and lipstick openly worn was a great advance from the furtive experiments that were all she had dared before then. From this, she was seized by an eagerness to expand her experience in other ways; and Peter, it seemed, was quite willing to accept this situation.

Instead of just walking and talking together, they began to go to the theater, to the cinema, even, occasionally, to a dance hall. But these new ventures, she found, were not always as enjoyable as she had expected. Peter was sometimes scornful of her opinions on the films and plays they saw. When they went dancing, he was annoyed by the attention attracted by her high spirits, and even more annoyed when other young men asked her to dance.

Peter, in fact, was also changing. Peter was becoming more and more critical in all of his attitudes towards her. But strangely, it was at the same time as he showed this new prickly side of himself that he also began to kiss her in the way Hughie had kissed. Yet still not exactly in that way . . .

There was one thing, Bridie realized, that she had learned from the experience with Hughie. She had learned to expect the sudden tumult of feeling that had momentarily carried her away, and so now she could anticipate and control its effect on her. And Peter did not hold her as closely as Hughie had done. His kisses were more restrained than Hughie's had been. And so Peter, she now realized also, must be practicing the same control. But there was still one thing she did not realize, and that was the way matters would come to a head between them when someone else got mixed up in all these changed circumstances.

The someone was Eric Faulkner, and it was towards the end of March that Bridie met him again.

One moment she was walking across the lobby of the North British Hotel to help Uncle George with a decorating job. The next she had cannoned into a broad back hidden from her by the huge sheaf of flowers in her arms. And there was Eric Faulkner, on his knees helping her to pick up the flowers, laughing and saying, my God it is, it *is* the little blond girl who can circle waltz, and where have you hidden yourself all this time, and look, couldn't you possibly get rid of all this pretty foliage somewhere, and give me the pleasure of looking at your pretty face, instead, over tea in the lounge here?

Tea in the magnificence of the North British lounge, with waiters hovering, and delicious little iced cakes, and cress sandwiches thin as wafers—it had been a treat impossible to resist! And Uncle George hadn't minded one bit, either. Uncle George, in fact, had been quite impressed by the casual elegance of this big, loose-limbed young man with his cultivated voice and imperious gestures to the waiting staff. And later, when Eric had offered to run her back to the shop in the open-topped red sports car parked near the hotel, Uncle Geroge had been perfectly happy about that too.

But Peter hadn't been happy. Peter had sulked and scowled his way through a whole evening after she'd told him about meeting Eric Faulkner—as if there was any harm in her just having tea with a bloke, Bridie thought indignantly; and parted from Peter that night with the thought that she *would* accept Eric's invitation to go out with him next Wednesday, on the shop's early closing day.

On Wednesday morning the shop phone rang. Eric's voice at the other end invited her to confirm their tentative arrangement; and by two o'clock that afternoon his sports car was rushing them through the green peace of of the countryside east of Edinburgh, past small white cottages huddled down under their roofs of glowing red pantiles, past fields with the green of barley already so high in them that they rolled away in all directions like—like—

Smooth, fertile sweeps of inland sea . . . The line Bridie needed for the poem she would make about the rich, rolling look of those fields came suddenly to her mind, and she chanted it aloud into the wind blowing her hair straight out behind her.

"What?" Eric shouted.

Shouting back, she told him, "It's a line of a poem; a poem *I'm* making."

"You?" He laughed his big, open laugh, and half turned to bellow something complimentary about his having known from the start that she was more than a pretty face.

When they stopped to have tea in one of the small villages on their way, he was even more complimentary, but all in such a teasing way that it did no more than exhilarate her into a verbal sparring match with him.

"You don't have a care in the world, do you?" she accused at last. And cheerfully he admitted:

"Not one. It comes of having been born with a silver spoon in my mouth, I suppose. But I can't help that, can I? And it is rather nice, you know, to be so certain of always getting one's own way."

He smiled at her, his usual smile of such complete self-assurance that Bridie could not help but laugh at him. He was an ass, she thought, but such a charming ass that it was difficult not to be taken with him. All the same . . . Half serious again, she warned:

"You'll trip up over that certainty yet, Eric."

Again that smile, but with something distinctly admiring in it this time. "With you, perhaps? Is that what you mean?"

"Yes, if you must know. With me."

"Let's wait and see, shall we?" His smile had broadened into the laugh that made his nature seem so frank, and Bridie was embarrassed by this. He had only been teasing again, she thought, and so the warning note she had sounded had made her seem a bit of a fool. Lightly in reply, she said:

"Why not?"

"Then here's to the future!" Laughing again, he led

the way back to the car; and as she followed him, Bridie asked herself, why not indeed? It was fun being with him, dashing about in his sporty little car, sparring over all the joking compliments he paid—the kind of fun she'd never had before. And so why shouldn't she go on taking advantage of it?

"Because you're making yourself cheap, that's why," Peter gave his own answer to her self-questioning. "Going out with anyone that asks you!"

"But Eric's not just anyone," she protested, then was shocked by the ugly expression that came over Peter's face and the harshness of the voice that retorted:

"You're right. He's a bad lot. A bounder. But of course, he's a well-heeled bounder—which has its own attraction, I suppose."

"That's a rotten way to talk!" Bridie bit her lip on the rest of the reply she would have liked to make, and stood wondering why she had ever thought that jealousy from Peter would be dangerous to her. To talk like that about a pleasant fellow like Eric—it was only making her angry! But it would still be a mistake, a terrible mistake, to give further rein to her anger, or Peter and she would never get back to their old footing with one another. And she *liked* Peter so much—never mind the amount she owed him in the way of friendship! As mildly as she could manage, Bridie said:

"You've got hold of the wrong end of the stick, Peter. It doesn't matter to *me* whether Eric has money or not. You should know me well enough by this time to

177

realize that. But you hardly know him from Adam, and so how can you say he's a bounder?"

Peter made no answer. He stood staring from the point where they had stopped at the top of the long flight of steps leading down from the Assembly Hall to the Art Gallery; staring, staring, as if the neoclassic bulk of the Gallery was the only thing of importance in the world to him. Bridie watched his profile and unwillingly remembered Nell speaking of the sixth sense that had warned of "a hard streak" in the nature of this very romantic-looking young man.

The hardness, she thought, was really showing itself now, in this argument over Eric Faulkner. But she could wear it down, couldn't she? Or at least she could try to do that. She made the effort, harking back to the theme of Eric's character.

"And anyway," she pointed out, "even if you are right and he is a bounder, that's the sort of thing I have to find out for myself, isn't it? You can't do my learning for me, after all, Peter."

Still not looking at her, Peter asked, "Has he kissed you?"

"Of course not!" Once again she was shocked. It was one thing, wasn't it, to spend an amusing hour or so with Eric Faulkner; but to share her kisses between him and Peter— With anger rising again in spite of herself, she spoke the end of her thought aloud. "What d'you think I *am*?"

Peter ignored the question, and asked one of his own. "Has he invited you out again?"

"Yes," she admitted. "He has. But honestly, Peter,

I can't see why you're making such a fuss over him. You were working on Wednesday, after all. You couldn't have taken me out then anyway. And what's more—" Now it was Moira's remark that came back to her, Moira asking satirically, *Where d'you think he spent his time before he met you? In a monastery?* "—you've been out plenty of times with other girls, haven't you?"

"Not since I met *you* again!" Peter's head jerked round to her, his eyes glaring and more brilliant than she had ever seen them before, even in the heat of their fiercest arguments. "And get this through your thick head, Bridie McShane. If I say you're not to go out with that fellow again, you won't!"

"Don't talk like that!" Involuntarily, Bridie backed a step. "You don't own me, Peter."

"Don't *you* talk like that!" Peter's hand shot out and clamped around her wrist. "You're my girl. You *do* belong to me."

"I belong to myself!" Bridie's answer was a cry that burst from her in the same second as she gave the violent jerk that freed her wrist. Panting with the effort, she stood nursing the wrist and trying to restrain the impulse that urged her to turn and run away from Peter. His eyes were still on her when she looked up, hostile eyes, as brilliant as ever. His mouth was still white at the corners with the rage that had gripped him. But she had control of her emotions now, and could speak quietly when she said:

"You shouldn't have said that, Peter. I know how you feel about my going out with Eric—at least, I

179

think I do. But—" She hesitated, seeking for some way to tone down the force of that cry of self-assertion, and Peter leapt into the gap of her hesitation.

"Then show respect for my feelings!"

She nodded. "All right. If you respect mine. Don't act as if I were a—a piece of property you'd somehow acquired."

Peter stood for a moment, biting his lip; and when he spoke at last, she realized that he too was making an effort to be reasonable.

"Maybe you're right," he admitted. "Maybe I did put it badly. I don't own you. Of course I don't. But—" He paused, as if to choose his words as carefully as possible, and then went on, "But I'm older than you. You're very inexperienced. You're—"

"That doesn't mean I'm stupid!"

Peter brushed aside the interruption. "You're unsophisticated about all sorts of things—including the fact that Eric Faulkner happens to be a type that can be recognized a mile away. And *that's* why I'm telling you that you're not to go out with him again."

"*Telling* me?"

"That's right." The truculent note was back in his voice. With a feeling of despair beginning to take hold of her, she protested:

"But Peter, you can't tell me what I must or mustn't do. My life is *my* life. And I'm the only one who can make the decisions in it."

"If you do go out with him again," Peter began, but she interrupted him there, telling him:

"Don't, Peter!"

180

"Don't what?"

"Make threats. Because that's what you were going to do, wasn't it? And it's not worthwhile, is it, to speak like that over something so harmless as being invited to a poetry lecture?"

"A poetry lecture!" Peter laughed without any amusement. "That's a new line, isn't it?"

"Well—" Bridie did her best to ignore the sarcasm. "It'll be new to me, at least. It's next week, in the Student Union—Professor Edwards on 'The Structure of the Sonnet.' And you know I've never had the chance to hear a lecture from a real Professor of Poetry."

Peter said sharply, "Don't try to confuse the issue. Are you going there with Faulkner or are you not?"

"I hadn't decided. But now you're forcing my hand, aren't you?"

"Not any more than you're forcing mine." Peter's gaze bored into hers. "And so listen, Bridie. I forbid you to go."

"You can't. You've already admitted you were mistaken to take that line with me."

"Oh, you can argue very well!" Peter's voice was bitter. "You have such a glib tongue on you. Always such a glib tongue!"

"That's not fair. I'm only trying to stand up for my rights."

Peter's eyes remained fixed on hers. Peter's will remained locked with her own. And neither—with a terrible sinking at the heart, Bridie knew it—neither would yield. Peter spoke at last, in a voice of chilling intensity.

"Think what you like about that. But do without me in future."

His right hand reached up to his hat—his wonderfully rakish-looking hat that he loved so much to wear, that suited him so well. He stepped back with the hand gripping the brim, and swept the hat off to bow briefly to her. Then he turned from her to the long flight of steps descending to the Art Gallery and ran down them, ran lightly and so fast that the slightest stumble would have sent him flying to break his neck at the foot of them.

Bridie watched with her mind momentarily closed to everything except the danger in such a lightning descent. Peter reached the foot of the steps and walked away without so much as a backwards glance at her, but she did not see which direction he took, because it was only with his safe arrival on level ground that the impact of his leaving really struck home. And when that happened, she was too blind with tears to see anything.

Part Three

19

Granda Armstrong stood outside the door between the drawing room and the small room where Granny Armstrong had lain ever since the beginning of the illness that had brought Bridie's mother to stay at Comiston as her nurse. With one hand, Granda opened the door of the sickroom. With the other, he flicked open his big gold watch.

"It's nearly time," he called.

Bridie's mother came out of the sickroom, leaving the door open behind her, and went to sit on the drawing-room couch beside William. She looked tired, Bridie thought. It hadn't been easy for her, finally having to decide she must give up the little house in the village where all her children had been born. And nursing a heavy woman like Granny Armstrong wasn't easy either. With a shiver against the morning chill

185

still hanging over the room, Bridie huddled closer into her chair beside the fire. She ought to have put on some warm clothes, she told herself, instead of coming downstairs in her dressing gown just because Sunday morning meant there was no real need to dress early.

"You will all be completely silent now," Granda Armstrong ordered.

A hush fell over the drawing room. Granda compared the time on his watch with that shown by the marble clock on the mantelpiece. Two seconds away from 11:15 A.M. Granda advanced to the radio in the window corner. From the sickroom where Granny Armstrong lay listening for the news they were all expecting, there came a creak of bedsprings. As that sound died, Granda switched on the radio. It was exactly 11:15 A.M. on Sunday the 3rd of September, 1939, and Prime Minister Chamberlain was about to speak to the nation.

The calm voice of the station announcer filled the drawing room. Then came the one they were all waiting for: an old man's voice with a sound that seemed as feeble and inconsequent as the buzzing of the few bees left in some worn-out hive.

Buzz buzz . . . The voice was talking about the attack Germany had launched two days ago on Poland. *Buzz buzz* . . . About the British and French treaty that had guaranteed Poland's safety against invasion. *Buzz buzz* . . . About the British and French ultimatum to Germany to withdraw its troops. *Buzz buzz* . . . About the ultimatum having now expired.

It seemed to Bridie that she was hearing all the

words spoken by that weary old voice as if they were no more than a scattered sequence of those bees hesitantly taking wing. A final bee buzz, a pause while Granda switched off the radio, and then they were all left looking at one another with the last words of the announcement still in their hearing.

This country is now at war with Germany.

It wasn't real, Bridie thought. It hadn't sounded real. It couldn't *be* real. All this talk of war against Germany—it had been going on again for months past, after all; ever since she had seen Peter for the last time, in fact, away back in March. It couldn't be real now, could it, just because some old man had said it was so?

Her mother and grandfather were deep in conversation, gloomily rehearsing the war talk all over again. Hitler, they were agreed, had never meant to keep his promises over Czechoslovakia. And once he had gobbled up the whole of that country, hadn't he made it obvious that Poland would be the next victim—all that propaganda he had put out, all those threats he had made? And now, of course, it was obvious that he hadn't believed the British and the French would honor their agreement to guarantee Poland's safety. That was the awful, the tragic part of it—the way he'd gone ahead with an attack that had *forced* this war on them.

It made sense, Bridie told herself, and yet it didn't make sense. Because a war couldn't happen in *her* life, could it? Not to her, not to Bridie McShane who had so much living to do yet!

Still with the feeling of existing within some incident that was totally unreal, she looked across at William. He had been following the conversation, it seemed, and he looked both puzzled and a little scared by it. It would be a good idea, she told herself, to take the kid out somewhere. He hadn't made all that many new friends, after all, since he'd had to leave the village and go to school in Edinburgh. But there was no need to hurry over going out, and so first of all she could have a bath.

Bridie rose to go upstairs, and once in the bath with her clothes lying ready beside it, she tried to decide where she should take William. They could make a whole day of their outing, she decided; take sandwiches and wander around in the Pentland Hills. It was easy enough to get to the Pentlands from Comiston, and—

An ear-splitting din bursting over the house brought her sitting bolt upright in the bath and then scrambling out of it, slipping and falling in her haste. A siren! My God, an *air-raid* siren. And the war still wasn't much more than ten minutes old! But there had been no air-raid drill yet—not for people in Edinburgh, at least. And what were you supposed to *do* in an air raid—no shelter to go to, like the one the Millers next door had in their garden, nowhere to hide—

With fingers that shook almost uncontrollably, Bridie pulled clothes on over her damp body, tugging, and weeping tearless sobs of frustration as the material stuck, and clung to her skin. But still nothing of it was real, any more than the radio announcement had been real. Air raids happened to other people, to people in Poland being dive-bombed by Stukas. But not to her, not to her, not to *her*! Still tugging at the skin-clinging folds of her dress, she dashed downstairs yelling, "William! William!" and ran straight out of the open front door, into the street.

William was there. Her mother, her grandfather were there. Half the people in Comiston were there, all of them staring skywards. She clutched William, and stared along with the others, all her sight concentrated on the fact that the cloudless blue above was still empty of planes, while intermittently her hearing took in scraps of the talk and excited speculation going on all around her.

. . . so soon! So soon after the declaration! . . . Blitzkrieg—"lightning war." That's what the Germans call it. They're launching a blitzkrieg on us, same as they've done to the Poles. . . . Forth Bridge—that's what they're after now! Bombing the Bridge . . . and Redford Barracks, of course. . . . Naval Dockyard at Rosyth. I bet it's the dockyard they're after. . . .

A siren again—the long, sustained note of the "All Clear" instead of the up-and-down banshee wailing of the warning siren, and everyone saying jubilantly:

"A test! That's all it was. They were just testing the sirens!"

Unreal, Bridie thought as she and William went back to the house. In spite of that trembling terror as she had tried to drag on her clothes, it was still all completely unreal. And tomorrow, when she went back to work in the shop, everything would be normal again.

Her mind stretched out to Monday morning, to the

wedding bouquets she had to make, to Hughie driving her in the van to the station so that they could put the bouquets on the ten-past-ten train for Dunbar. The rest of Sunday, it began to seem to her, was just a period to be got through till then, a sort of hallucination that had inexplicably been created out of those few, ridiculous words spoken by some weary old man far away in London. And the hallucination would vanish as quickly as it had occurred because wars, the disbelieving voice in her mind kept repeating, just *couldn't* happen in her life!

At ten o'clock on Monday morning, the truth finally broke on Bridie.

For several minutes before that time, the van with Hughie and herself in it had been part of a traffic jam making noisy confusion of the west entrance to the Waverley Station—the narrow downward slope they called the Carriage Drive. In the back of the van lay the bouquets for the out-of-town wedding, but there would be no hope of getting those delivered on time if they could not break free of the jam with at least a few minutes to spare before the ten-past-ten train drew out. Bridie decided on the only course that seemed sensible.

"Switch off, Hughie," she ordered. "If we take a chance on leaving the van here, I can run ahead with the bride's bouquet and get the guard to hold up the train while you follow on with that pile of bouquets for the bridesmaids."

"Right!" Hughie was only too happy to have their

190

problem taken out of his hands. They scrambled from the van. Bridie seized the bride's bouquet, and started off down the pavement lining the slope of the Carriage Drive. The bouquet was fragile. The pavement was narrow and crowded. She had to be careful to shield the long sheaf of flowers from the press of the throng. In her preoccupation with this, she was only vaguely aware that there were as many soldiers as civilians attempting to make their way out of the station. She reached the end of the Carriage Drive, turned into the main concourse of the station, and stopped dead in her tracks.

The concourse was jammed with figures, hopelessly jammed by a solid mass of khaki-clad men. And the platforms beyond the concourse were also jammed. The station was full, as chock-full as it could be, of soldiers—fresh-faced young men in stiff, new-looking uniforms, NCO's with the hard-bitten look of the professional soldier; officers with brass shoulder pips and leather belts gleaming.

The war was real!

The force of the fact hitting home held Bridie standing there like someone petrified. The bouquet in her hand was buffeted by one figure after another crowding past her. The bouquet was disintegrating into a mess of broken flowers and headless stems, and although she felt the blows that were destroying it, she could not have moved to prevent them, supposing her life had depended on it.

Everything in her, every emotion, every thought, every feeling, had concentrated on that one sharp realization. *The war was real!* And it was mad! All those men going out to fight, to die; it was mad, utterly mad! A shout rose inside her, a shout of violent, despairing anger:

"Go home! You fools, go home, go home!"

Her vocal nerves had shared in the paralysis that gripped her. She could neither form the shout nor utter it, and it was Hughie who eventually broke the spell—Hughie arriving half smothered in a pile of bridesmaids' bouquets and panting to a halt with the question:

"Y' a' right, hen?"

Bridie had no need to look at the bouquet in her hand to know what had happened to it, but she looked all the same, and said shakily:

"I'm okay. But this is ruined."

"Ach, so what! Ah've got a' these here. The bride c'n take one o' them."

Hughie was irrepressibly cheerful as usual, even more than usual, Bridie realized. He was glancing exultantly around the mass in the concourse, and there was an almost electric excitement coming out of him as he added.

"An' the minute Ah get this lot on the train, Ah'm for the Army!"

The second part of that morning's truth hit Bridie then. *Peter!* Peter would be caught up in the war— maybe already *was* caught up in it!

"Make for the train with those bouquets," she told Hughie. "I've something more urgent to do now."

She turned from him on her last word, and began

192

to force her way out of the station. In the phone box at the top of the Carriage Drive slope, she put down the ruined bouquet and dialed the number of Peter's firm. A brisk voice at the other end asked what she wanted. She put the question burning in her mind, and the brisk voice instructed:

"Hold on. I'll have the records checked." A wait that seemed endless before the operator was back to her, and then, "You're quite right. We did have a Peter McKinley on the books. But he's left the job. On August tenth, according to Personnel."

"Left?" Bridie stood stupidly for a moment with the phone to her ear. Then, hurriedly, in case the operator rang off, she asked, "Will you put me through to the machine shop, please."

There was clicking and ringing at the other end, a man's voice answering, a sound of machinery clattering through her own first words. The man's voice shouted:

"Hold on till I get this damn door shut." The machinery noise was abruptly cut off, and the man's voice said, "Jack Taylor here. What's your problem, miss?"

"I want to know about Peter McKinley, Mr. Taylor."

"What d'you mean, you 'want to know'? He's left here. Left away back in August."

"Yes, I've been told that. But why did he leave? Was it—did he leave to join the Forces?"

"You're damn right he did!" Jack Taylor sounded suddenly envious. "The Navy. They've been crying out for blokes with his kind of skill. But, here—" The envious note changed suddenly to one of suspicion. "What's this all about, eh? What's *your* right to ask questions about Peter?"

"I'm his girl." Bridie hadn't meant to say that, but the unexpected suspicion drew the words defensively out of her. They made Jack Taylor laugh before he said:

"I see. I see now. You had a fight with him, eh? And he rushed off to join the Navy. And here were all us lads thinking he was just keen to get in a crack at Hitler! Ach well—" The amused tone gave way to a consoling one. "Not to worry, hen. It'll all be over by Christmas."

Over by Christmas. They had prophesied the same thing at the start of the last war, her father and mother's war that had lasted for four years and killed four million men! Bridie felt an impulse to slam down the receiver. But there was some barrier against this in her mind, an area of numbness where the impulse died before it could be translated into action.

Politely, instead, before she hung up, she took leave of Jack Taylor as if they had just had an ordinary conversation on an ordinary day. Then she gathered up the rest of the bouquet and went back into the station to look for Hughie; walking slowly, the broken sheaf of flowers trailing from one hand as she walked, and in her mind the confused feeling that she was now also trailing with her some broken part of her own life.

194

20

People began to notice that there was something wrong with Bridie.

"Is she sulking?" Jemima asked. "I've never known her do that, before. But she's gone so quiet!"

Worriedly her mother added, "And so listless, too."

Granny Armstrong roused herself from her sickbed to recommend a dose of Gregory's. Bunty came into the shop to show off her new baby, and said in her usual forthright way that Bridie looked like something the cat had brought home. Granda Armstrong complained about the amount of his October electricity bill, and ordered her to stop burning her bedroom light to such unearthly hours. Mr. Finkelstein, when he came in for his roses, took to remarking how pale she had become. But Mr. Finkelstein was more astute than the others. Mr. Finkelstein guessed she had problems; and when she was on her way home from the shop one evening, he called to her from the doorway of his own shop:

"A minute, *mein Kind*! Just a minute of your time."

Bridie followed as he went back into his shop. He was just on the point of closing, it seemed, and he let down the catch on his door before he led the way into the back shop.

"Your mama's locket," he explained. "One more little thing I have to do to the clasp, and then you can take it home with you."

The locket hung by its chain from one of the hooks on a velvet-covered board on the wall of his back shop. Mr. Finkelstein lifted it down to begin working on the clasp, talking all the time he did so. And very soon, as so often happened with him, it was the war he spoke about. But Mr. Finkelstein wasn't like other people now when he spoke about the war.

Other people, at first, had been as shocked as he was by the German invasion of Poland. Other people had been just as appalled by the carnage in bombed cities, the merciless scattering of the Polish defenses. But that was all over now. Poland was conquered. And for the rest of Europe, the war had become no more than a matter of waiting for Hitler to decide on his next move. A "phoney war," all those others called it, and went around grumbling about the way it meant having to put up with food rationing and carrying gas masks and identity cards and buying material for blackout curtains against the air raids that still hadn't happened.

But Mr. Finkelstein didn't grumble. Mr. Finkelstein was forever warning, instead, that the so-called defensive line in France could easily be bypassed through Holland and Belgium, that Hitler would have no conscience about violating the neutrality of these two countries. Most of all, Mr. Finkelstein warned, Hitler was busily regrouping all his forces for that very purpose, and there would be a terrible price to pay yet for this period of phoney war.

Bridie began deliberately to tune Mr. Finkelstein's voice out of her hearing in the same way as she was becoming used to tuning out the voices of those who grumbled. But she wasn't doing so, she assured herself, because she didn't believe what he was saying. How could she fail to believe, in fact, when her mind was still so sharply imprinted with that terrible moment of realizing that the war *was* real? Yet even Mr. Finkelstein accepted that Hitler's next attack in Europe wasn't likely to take place until next spring, and she could think about that when it came. But meanwhile she had other things to worry about, and so meanwhile also, it was only when people spoke about the war at sea that she really listened to them.

At sea there were packs of German submarines always lying with torpedo tubes loaded for attack on the merchant ships that had to cross the Atlantic. At sea the Navy was fighting back against the U-boat wolf packs, shepherding the slow merchantmen in convoy, constantly patrolling the deep gray waters

197

that could, at any second, explode with death. At sea that terrible reality of war was still always present— and why, oh why did it have to be the Navy that Peter had joined!

"You are very silent," Mr. Finkelstein told her. "And I? It may be that I talk too much because I have such dread of the terrible things that have still to happen in Europe. But now—" With a shrug, and a wry smile at himself, he tidied away his kit of delicate little tools and picked up the locket. "Now I tell you how much better it is to create than to destroy. And so I must tell you also that this trinket here I have with my own hands made. Long ago, for your father to give to your mother to celebrate their *Heiraten*—no, no, I am using the wrong word! *Heiraten* is 'getting married,' and this was for their engagement—see!"

A flick of his long, clever fingers opened the locket's heart-shaped case of gold. Two faces looked out from photographs set inside the case: the gentle one of a smiling, dark-haired young woman, the composed and rather stern face of a man with smooth, fair hair. Bridie found she had the locket in her hand and was studying the faces.

Had her mother ever looked so young? As for her father, she thought, it was strange after so many years of grieving for him to find she could look at him now with tenderness rather than with pain! She laid the locket back on the worktable, conscious of Mr. Finkelstein's eyes on her, but carefully avoiding any answering look or word when he said jovially:

"And perhaps for you and your young man, some-day, I will make another locket, *ja*?"

There was a small rustling of tissue paper as he began wrapping up the locket, a silence while she sat staring at her feet; and then his voice again, very gentle and coaxing:

"You are not sulking as they say you are, *mein Kind*. You are sad. Is this not so?"

Still she stared at her feet, and still she did not give even a nod or shake of the head in answer. Why should she, after all, when any kind of an answer might finish up by trapping her into the horrible admission that Jack Taylor had maybe been right? That maybe she *had* been responsible for Peter rushing off to volunteer as Hughie had done instead of waiting to be called up along with the others in his age-group?

The voice came again, the same coaxing voice. "*Ach*, this is not good for you, not good at all. Tell me, *mein Liebling*. Tell Papa Finkelstein."

Bridie found her eyes filling suddenly with tears. It had been that "Papa" bit that had broken her, she realized. And the gentle voice, the voice her own father had always used when he knew very well she had been burdened by some awful secret. She mopped away her tears, not realizing in her distracted state of mind that she was using the white linen polishing cloth on Mr. Finkelstein's worktable. But he noticed and laughed a little. And from that, it was an easy step to laughing at herself and so regaining her composure.

"There isn't much to it really," she began then.

"Peter—my young man, as you call him—Peter and I were good friends. Then we quarreled, and I haven't seen him or even heard from him since then."

"Oh come now," Mr. Finkelstein persuaded. "Many girls and young men have such quarrels. It is not so serious!"

"It is for me. He went off to join the Navy—sometime in August, I think. And I don't even know now if—if—" Bridie found herself stammering helplessly for a moment, but still the words she had only dared to think before insisted on being said. "—if he's alive or dead," she finished, and was taken aback then to see Mr. Finkelstein beginning to smile again.

"There," he said briskly, "I can reassure you. Your young man will have to be trained before he is sent to sea, and so first of all that will mean three, four—maybe as much as five months for him at some shore base. But tell me now. What was this quarrel about? Some other young man, perhaps?" Bridie looked away from him, aware that the flush on her face had already given an answer to his question, and Mr. Finkelstein was tactful enough to let her color die away before he pursued, "And you are even more sad over the quarrel, perhaps, because this other young man was not worth it?"

Eric Faulkner hadn't been worth a damn! Involuntarily, as she remembered the occasion at the Student Union, Bridie grew tight-lipped with anger again. Eric Faulkner had been so charmingly, so *falsely* apologetic over "making a mistake" in the date of the poetry lecture—the nonexistent poetry lecture! But it was

200

only afterwards, of course, that she had discovered how he had lied to her about it, after she had discovered how often he had already invented some such occasion to lure earnest idiots like herself into the Student Union first, and then into the lounge-bar there. And then, when a few drinks had made the poor fool muzzy, into that ghastly, bewildering maze of corridors and the room to which he so conveniently had a key!

"The other young man," she said aloud, "was a bounder, a thoroughly bad lot. And I hope he roasts in hell!"

"*Ach, mein Gott!*" Mr. Finkelstein was alarmed at the violence of her tone. "He did you harm?"

"No. He didn't get that satisfaction." *The red-headed student—the girl who had tipped her the wink in the ladies' loo* . . . "He meant to, but"—Bridie gave a grim little laugh—"another girl warned me in time about him. And then it was the oddest thing, Mr. Finkelstein—" She paused again, remembering how unbelieving of the girl student she had been; and then, when the girl took off in a huff, how she had decided to play it safe anyway, and had got lost for her pains in that same maze of corridors.

"It was the oddest thing," she repeated. "I thought I was lost, done for, caught in the very trap he'd set for me. Then I ran across this big, fat woman cleaner, mopping away at the floor of the corridor I was wandering in. *And I knew her!*"

Fat Liz bent over her cleaner's bucket! Fat Liz looking up, uncomprehending for a moment, at the stranger questioning her; then the mutual recognition, the cries of "Bridie, hen! What's wrong?" and "Liz, oh Liz, I'm so glad to see you!"

"I knew her from the time we happened to be in the hospital together," Bridie went on, "and she rescued me. In fact—" She laughed again, a laugh of genuine pleasure this time. "She not only showed me the way out of the place, she took me home to supper with her, and I met her husband and all her kids, and we had an uproarious time reminiscing about the hospital."

"She sounds to me," Mr. Finkelstein remarked, "like a very fine person."

"The finest!" Bridie emphasized. "She's a big woman, Mr. Finkelstein. Carries herself like a Queen. And that's how she *was* to me that night."

Mr. Finkelstein smiled, indulging her enthusiasm, and then said cautiously, "But Bridie, *mein Kind*, if this other young man was such a—what did you call him?—was such a 'bounder,' were you not wrong to quarrel over him with your own young man, your Peter?"

"Mr. Finkelstein"—Bridie found a lump rising in her throat and had to stop to swallow it down—"I can't tell you how many times I've asked myself that question. But the answer is still always, no, I wasn't wrong. I didn't know Faulkner was a bounder, after all. And neither did Peter. That was something I had to find out for myself. But Peter didn't want it that way, because—"

202

"Because, of course, he was jealous," Mr. Finkelstein interrupted, and impatiently she agreed:

"Yes, yes, I could see that. And I could understand it too. But don't *you* see, Mr. Finkelstein? Peter had no right to forbid me to see this other fellow. And *that* was the rock we split on. Peter and I were friends. We weren't committed to one another in any other way. And now—"

"Now," Mr. Finkelstein interrupted again, "now I think you are. Is that not so?"

Were they? Was she really justified in thinking that Peter could have rushed off to the war just because of the way he felt about her? Was she so miserable now because she had the same feeling for him?

Helplessly Bridie said, "I don't know if that's so or not, Mr. Finkelstein. I don't really know."

"Hmmm." Mr. Finkelstein sat stroking his dark, heavy chin. "We have a problem, no? You are unhappy, that is clear. But there must be a way to make you happy. Tell me—" The shrewd eyes above the caressing hand shot a glance at Bridie. "How have you spent your time since you parted from your Peter?"

"Work." Bridie shrugged. "I just work more than I ever did before."

"No, no!" Mr. Finkelstein waved away her answer. "I am not talking about the flower shop, about your job."

Bridie stared at him. "But neither am I! My job is just something to give me a living. That's how it's always been with me. My work, my real work, is my writing."

"*Ach, so!*" Mr. Finkelstein looked startled. "Your grandfather has said to me how always in your room at night you scribble, scribble. But this I did not know, that for you writing is serious."

"You should see my room," Bridie told him. "I could paper the walls with the manuscripts I've got there."

"But this is interesting!" Mr. Finkelstein settled back to look at her with wonder in his face. "Always it is interesting to come across the creative spirit. But tell me—" He paused to cough delicately behind his hand, as if to apologize in advance for his question. "—you have, perhaps, published some of your work?"

Bridie shook her head. "I did try once. But I know now I was wrong to do that. I think I've probably got a long way to go yet before I'm at that stage."

"You are sensible." Mr. Finkelstein nodded approval. "You have learned the first lesson of experience. But permit me. There is one thing more I must ask. In all this writing since you quarreled with your young man, has there ever been a letter to him?"

"No." Bridie shook her head. "When we quarreled, it was he who left me. If I would not agree with him, he said, I must do without him in future."

"*Ach!*" Mr. Finkelstein sighed. "So headstrong are young men! No tact. No diplomacy. No thought of the regrets to come!"

"But I don't know if he *has* regretted it!" Bridie exclaimed. "That's the real problem, Mr. Finkelstein. And so how *could* I go running after him now?"

"Who spoke of running after him?" Mr. Finkelstein demanded. "And what is your skill in words for if you cannot use it to discover what he now feels for you?"

"No!" Bridie met the questions with an even more vehement shake of the head. "It wouldn't matter how I put it, Mr. Finkelstein, it would still sound like a begging letter."

"Then send him a sign of some kind!" Mr. Finkelstein cried. "Use the oldest language in the world, you foolish little one. Send him some token that will say *you* have not changed, even if he has. Then you will not have to sound like a beggar. And he, if he has not changed, will be able to tell you so by sending some token in return."

With a quick little gesture he pushed the wrapped locket towards Bridie. "Here," he said. "Here is one token that has served its purpose. Now you find one that will serve yours."

Bridie's hand closed over the small, hard shape of the locket. She stood up, aware that she had been dismissed, but with a question still in her mind. Suppose there was no token from Peter in return, what then? Hesitantly she voiced her question.

"Then," Mr. Finkelstein answered, "you will at least know that all is finally over so far as he is concerned. And it will be better to know that, will it not, than to go on with the uncertainty you have now?"

There was something in the tone of his voice that brought Bridie out of her preoccupation with herself. She looked wonderingly at him, and realized that his mind had drifted far away from her, as it had done that day his hands had bled from their grip on the thorny rose stems. He sat with those hands in front of him now, their fingers tightly interlocked—soft jeweler's hands, the hands of a Jew who could have relatives and friends among the other Jews suffering and dying at that very moment in the ghettos of conquered Polish cities; loved ones whose fate he would never know for certain . . .

Awkwardly Bridie reached out one of her own hands to cover his. He blinked, his gaze coming back from the middle distance to focus on hers; and quietly then, she said:

"I wish you could know too, Mr. Finkelstein. And I'm very grateful to you."

Mr. Finkelstein gave her a twisted little smile. *"Macht nichts,"* he said. "Think nothing of it." And heaved himself up then to show her, with all his usual gallantry, to the door.

21

Granny Armstrong was beginning to need nursing through the night as well as through the day. Bridie and her mother took turn and turn about in this, cat-napping on a couch beside the sickbed; and it was through the night, when she had to rise time and time again to tend the old lady, that Bridie thought most of the token she would send Peter.

It had seemed an easy enough idea to carry out when Mr. Finkelstein spoke of it—just to send the token to Peter's home in a wrapping marked "Please Forward." But what was the token itself to be? A gift of some kind, specially bought for the purpose? Peter would recognize her handwriting on the wrapping and be able to guess from that who had sent it. But a gift, she argued to herself, would amount to the same as writing a letter. It would be like a plea that said:

"Forgive me. Take me back." And that was not at all what she wanted to say.

Some personal possession, then? Something Peter would recognize as hers? There was that small green scarf of chiffon silk he had always liked to see her wear. And perhaps he could send her something of his own in return—*if* he wanted to reply, and *if* he had anything with him that would be the equivalent of her green scarf.

For a week of broken nights Bridie lay with one idea after another churning through her brain. But by the end of that time she was still no nearer an answer to her problem, and it was purely by chance on one night of the following week that she did find the answer.

She had taken a book downstairs with her that night, an anthology of verse—just the thing, she had thought, for brief spells of reading. She flicked the pages, half smiling occasionally at the sight of an old favorite and occasionally also feeling a pang at the heart when she came across some of the lines she and Peter had once enjoyed sharing with one another.

By the time she had reached the section headed "Irish Poets," she was thinking more and more of all the times she and Peter had talked as they walked together. And suddenly, there it was on the page before her—Peter's first choice among all those he had loved to quote, the one thing he could not fail to recognize as coming from her, the one token it would be right to send!

Bridie slid noiseless from her couch and padded off

to fetch writing materials from the desk in the drawing room. Granny Armstrong whimpered and stirred as she returned to sit down beside the small night lamp. The stirring ceased, and carefully she began to write:

Had I the heavens' embroidered cloths
Enwrought with gold and silver light,
The blue and the dim and the dark cloths
Of night and light and the half-light,

Granny Armstrong stirred again. She called out hoarsely, and Bridie rose to help her turn in bed. She settled the heavy form, smoothed the bedclothes, and sat down again before her half-completed copy of the poem.

Half-completed ... To send *only* this half—what better way could there be of testing Peter's feelings? She would know it was the end between them—wouldn't she?—if he ignored it. But if he chose to reply with the poem's other half ...

Her fingers shaking a little now, Bridie folded the paper with its four lines of poetry and sealed it into its envelope. If she posted it next morning to Peter's home, and if his mother forwarded it straight away to wherever he was, how soon could she expect his reply? What sort of delay did wartime conditions impose on the mails? And supposing his training was finished and he was finally away at sea—far away, perhaps, on a convoy run—how soon could she expect an answer then?

Bridie fell into a doze at last with the beat of *"How*

soon?" on her brain; and her mother was disturbed the next morning to see the dark rings of sleeplessness around her eyes. There was a family conference, with her mother defending Granny's stubborn refusal to be moved to hospital or to have a professional nurse, but still insisting that *something* had to be done about letting a girl of Bridie's age have enough sleep. And with Granny herself, of course, still pathetically saying it wasn't too much to ask, surely, to have her own daughter and granddaughter caring for her instead of being in the hands of a lot of strangers.

"All right then," Uncle George told them at last. "Bridie can work part time to let her catch up on sleep during the day. And I'll get Bunty to come back to the shop till Granny's better."

But Granny, they all knew, wasn't going to get better; and mixed with the tension of watching out for the mail each day, Bridie began also to feel the tension of a house with a dying person in it.

I would spread the cloths under your feet:
But I, being poor, have only my dreams;
I have spread my dreams under your feet;
Tread softly because you tread on my dreams.

Peter's answer, Peter's half of the token had taken more than four weeks to arrive. But she had it now, in his sprawling, almost illegible handwriting, and her happiness was springing up inside her like the spring of a lark into the sky on a clear day. And on the first opportunity she had after she read the lines, she told Mr. Finkelstein:

"I did it, Mr. Finkelstein! I sent a token, like you said, and now I've got the other half of it back from him!"

"Oh!" Mr. Finkelstein was broadly smiling. "So now all is joy! And when will you see him again?"

"I don't know." There had been nothing on the sheet of notepaper except those four lines. But that had been enough to tell her she *would* see him again, and so even in her admission there was joy and an assurance at the end of it. "But I will see him, Mr. Finkelstein. Quite soon, maybe, because we're almost at Christmas and the New Year. And it's customary to let Servicemen have leave then, isn't it?"

"Yes, yes, if they can be spared from their units, that is so. But meanwhile, Bridie—" Mr. Finkelstein's smiling face grew suddenly grave. "Other matters, I hear, are not going so well for your family. Your grandmother; soon, it seems, it will be time to say Kaddish for her."

Kaddish, the Jewish prayer for the dead . . . Bridie felt the vanishing of the smile on her own face, a stiffening of the features in the chill the word brought to her. Yet still she could not quite repress the bubbling-up of her own secret happiness, either then or when she was back in the little room that now had the smell of death in it; and where now also, in her share of night duty, she was sometimes even a little afraid to be alone with the muttering shape that had once been her brisk, managing Granny.

"But you're to call me, remember, the minute you see she's taking a turn for the worse," her mother instructed, and so she assured herself there was nothing to be afraid of really. Besides which, being disturbed from sleep at night didn't matter now that all it meant was a little more waking time to enjoy this wonderful feeling of happiness.

The paper with the four line of poetry on it became limp with all the times she had folded and unfolded it. The few days to Christmas slid past, then Christmas itself without a sign of Peter; and that was a disappointment. But there was still New Year to look forward to, and meanwhile she could read and re-read those four lines.

I have spread my dreams under your feet . . . and he had. Peter had a reserved nature, but he had never been reserved with her. Peter had talked often in a way that left him most vulnerable—

"Bridie! Bridie!" The old lady in the bed was getting restless again. Bridie rose to soothe her and then went back to her reading.

Tread softly because you tread on my dreams. Maybe—no, not maybe, but almost certainly she had been guilty of that in the quarrel over Eric Faulkner, and—

"Bridie!" The feeble voice coming from the bed had the querulous note that meant her grandmother urgently wanted something—a cool drink, a back rub, to be turned over in bed—it could be any one of a dozen things, Bridie thought resignedly. She slipped the paper into her pocket and went over to the bed.

"Yes, Granny?"

"What time is it?"

212

"Two A.M., Granny."

"No, no, I didn't mean that." Granny's voice creaked with irritation. "What's the date? What's the time of year?"

"December, Granny. Nearly the end of the month. The thirtieth."

"What happened to Christmas?"

"We just let it go by. You weren't well enough to have any fuss in the house."

"I can't sleep, Bridie." Granny Armstrong's eyes were like slits from the laudanum she had to take to smother her pain, and the laudanum should have made her sleepy. But sometimes she seemed deliberately to resist its effect, as if clinging to her waking moments meant she could cling to life, Bridie thought; and with a sudden rush of compassion for the old lady, she asked:

"Will I read to you, Granny?"

"No, no, no. Can't be bothered with reading. But sit where I can see you."

Obediently Bridie sat in the low chair beside the bed. Her grandmother's hand moved over the coverlet to rest on her own. Her grandmother's voice started up again, a muttering voice that talked inconsequently of this and that. Her mind was wandering, Bridie realized, going back and back over the years to her childhood, to her youth, to her time as a mother of young children, all of it mixed up and out of sequence.

I'd better call Mum. At the very moment the thought

passed through her mind, Bridie became aware of Granny Armstrong mentioning Peter's name. And there it was again! Something, something, "young McKinley."

"What did you say, Granny?" Bridie leaned closer to her grandmother, spoke slowly to be sure the old woman understood, and was startled to feel a sudden tightening of the grip in the hand holding her own.

"Young McKinley." The slitlike eyes opened wider on the words; the voice that spoke them had grown in strength. "That boy, Peter. I asked you, 'Do you love him?' "

What could she say? Granny was dying, and you had to speak the truth to someone who was dying. But what *was* the truth?

"I—I don't know, Granny." With difficulty, Bridie forced the words out. "I'm not sure yet, but I—I think I do."

There was a different look now in those half-open eyes fixed on her own, a look of desperation. And although she had never seen such a look before, Bridie recognized what it meant. Granny Armstrong had something to tell her, and Granny knew she had only seconds of her life left for the telling of that something.

"You must call Mum," Bridie instructed herself. Yet still she could not bear to remove that clutching hand. Still she could not take her eyes off those dying eyes. And now Granny was forming words again, words that came out in an intense half whisper.

"Hold on to love. This house—always—too much thought of money in it. Love—Love got lost. . . ." A pause, a last flaring of light in the eyes fixed on hers, a working of the withered lips. And then, suddenly clear as a bell, sounding half like a plea and half like a cry of exaltation, the last words of all:

"Oh, Bridie girl, hold on to love!"

22

It was on a blustery day of March sunshine that Bridie and Peter met again.

There had been no sign of him at the New Year, no further word either since the second four lines of the poem had arrived. But, Bridie reasoned to herself, she could understand why that was so. Hadn't she herself found it impossible to write any letter that wouldn't sound like an apology? And wasn't it better to leave everything that needed saying till it could be said face to face?

With the wind whipping at her hair as she walked away from the shop that day, she tried to decide how she would spend her afternoon. It was Wednesday, her one free afternoon of the week, and the thought of going out to walk in the Pentland Hills was a tempting one. In the hills would be the smell of wet moss and heather, the melancholy of curlews crying, the winding brown lines of sheep tracks fading into the distance—everything, in fact, that would help to capture the atmosphere she needed for one last stab at the tinker woman's story.

If she went up to the National Library, on the other hand, she would have all those free hours to make notes for the next part of her historical novel. At the Library, too, she'd be near enough the Old Town to walk around all the scenes of her book and feel them coming alive in her mind. And then, if she was lucky, she might be able to transfer that feeling to the pages of her work.

The novel won the contest. The novel was the most ambitious piece of writing she had yet attempted, and the thought of it always excited her. But first of all, she decided, she'd have to let her mother know she'd not be in that afternoon.

She turned the corner into Comiston and saw that the street ahead was empty save for the figure of a man advancing from the opposite direction—a young man, by the jauntiness of his walk; a Naval rating in the usual bell-bottom trousers and tight-fitting sailor jerkin, with his round, sailor's hat worn at a rakish tilt over one eye. *Worn at a rakish tilt . . .*

Bridie's heart began to beat as if she were running instead of allowing her steps to falter and slow almost to a halt. The sailor also slowed his pace. But only for a few steps; then it changed suddenly to a run, and it *was* Peter, and she was running too, and his hands were held out, and so were hers. And then they had met, and they were standing with hands clasping hands, smiling, giving little gasps of laughter, and she was saying:

"It was your hat—the way you tilt it. I didn't realize it was you till I noticed that."

"I'd called at the house and your mother said you were due home, but I wasn't sure it was you, either, till I saw the sun strike your hair. All in black"—Peter spread their clasped hands so that he could look her up and down—"just like a wee, old market wifie!"

"My Granny died."

"Oh, I'm sorry. I'm really sorry."

Their smiles had faded into seriousness. They stood looking at one another, each searching the other's face and matching memory with what they found there. Peter said:

"You haven't changed." His eyes flickered upwards to her hair. One hand followed the glance of his eyes. The hand gently stroked her hair as she told him:

"You haven't either. Except that you look even better as a sailor than you did as a civilian."

" 'Civvy.' " Peter's smile reappeared along with his correcting word. "You'll have to learn my slang now, Navy slang. Home is Civvy Street, and all the people at home are civvies. I'm a matelot—that's the slang for 'sailor,' and the Navy itself is 'the Andrew.' "

Bridie tried to match his smile as she asked, "And how long has the Andrew given you in Civvy Street?"

"Ten days," he told her. "And I have an awful lot

218

saved up to say to you—things that've been too difficult to put into letters."

"I'll ask my uncle to give me ten days off work," she said. "And if he says 'no,' I'll take them just the same."

Peter laughed. "You don't get any less rebellious, do you?" he asked, and slid an arm around her waist to walk her off with him through the sunshine that seemed to be blazing now with a light in it like the light of glory.

They walked that afternoon beside the pond in the Braid Park, where the wood now held masses of daffodils trumpeting their silent song, and primroses were scattered like the small, pale gold of fallen stars. Bridie found herself learning more naval slang and cautiously feeling her way through this to answers for the most important of the questions she had to ask.

"You're wondering why I joined up before I had to go," Peter said eventually. "Isn't that it?"

"More than wondering," Bridie confessed. "It's something I *have* to know."

"And it's something I *have* to tell." Peter drew her down to sit on the grass beside him. "D'you remember," he asked, "all those times we stood at The Mound, shouting up for the kind of things we believe in? Freedom, liberty of conscience—all the things you have to shout up for sometime if you're not going to lose them forever. Well, that was part of it, because it's those very things that Hitler and his mob are out to destroy. And I knew, of course, that the war would happen. That it *had* to happen, and pretty soon at that. Then there was you."

"Here it comes," Bridie thought. "Here it comes at last!" But it wouldn't be so bad, would it, now that she knew she wasn't entirely to blame for Peter's decision to join?

Peter reached out to take her hands in his. "I knew I'd have to go in a few months' time anyway," he said. "But you. You'd become entirely too much for me to handle by then. I went around wondering what I'd say to you if we met accidentally, afraid of meeting you, wanting that to happen, *not* wanting it. And so I ran away to give myself the chance to think things out. And I wish now I hadn't. I wish now I'd taken that chance of a few more months with you, because—"

He stopped abruptly and looked down at their interclasped hands. Then, just as abruptly, he freed Bridie's hands from his and rose to walk to the edge of the pond. A mallard drake began to swim inshore to him; maybe the same mallard, she thought, that they had fed so long ago at that very spot. She rose to join Peter at the water's edge, and with her heart thudding so hard that it made her breathless, she said:

"There's our mallard, Peter."

"—because now I've only got nine more left of my ten days," Peter went on with his sentence, and turned as he spoke to put his arms around her. "And that's not enough, Bridie. There never will be enough days for all the time I want with you."

The clasp of his arms tightened. He kissed her, and

it was like fire striking fire, like all the yearnings she had ever had being satisfied in one great rush of bliss. They drew apart, both of them trembling, and it was a moment or two before she could control her voice enough to say:

"We'll make the most of them, Peter."

23

They got the inevitable "duty" visits over as quickly as possible.

Uncle George fumed over Bridie's demand for time off, but grudgingly at last agreed to pay the price Bunty demanded for taking her place. Her mother sighed, and said,

"Well, I'm sure Peter's a fine young man. But you're young enough yet, aren't you, to go courting?"

Bridie blushed at that word "courting"; but Peter seemed to enjoy it, and calmly used it himself when he took Bridie to renew acquaintance with his own parents.

They looked in briefly on Peter's former workmates. Bridie discovered that the voice of Jack Taylor belonged to a sandy-haired young man who seemed delighted to meet her at last in person, and who embarrassed her by telling Peter openly that he'd found himself "a nice girl."

"That's your share of the compliments," Peter told her, grinning, and on impulse then, Bridie decided they should round off the day with a visit to Fat Liz.

"Because I think you ought to meet her," she said, and in spite of Peter's demands to know more than this, would explain no further. Liz, her instinct told her, would do all the explaining needed. Liz would seize on any chance to expound a drama that would clear up the last shadow lying between herself and Peter—the shadow of Eric Faulkner.

Liz was at home with all her brood, when they called, and with her husband John contentedly beaming on the result of his being allowed to exercise his "rights."

"Well, I never!" In a voice that rose to a shriek of amazed delight, she made even their entry as dramatic as Bridie could have wished. But the eyes that summed up Peter's appearance were shrewd, and it was not long before she was turning to tell Bridie:

"Your lad has an honest face, hen. And bonny eyes. Aye, bonny, bonny blue eyes. You've done well for yourself."

Peter asked teasingly, "So have I, don't you think?"

"I don't just think it," Fat Liz retorted. "I know it." Dramatically she struck her massive bosom. "Deep down here in my heart, I know it. She's a lass of spirit, this one!"

Bridie grinned at this, and reminded her, "You've

said that before about me, Liz. On the night you rescued me from Eric Faulkner, remember?"

"Do I not?" Liz rolled her eyes and made yet another expressive gesture before she settled down, as Bridie had guessed she would, to retell the tale. And there was nothing that Liz didn't know, of course, about trigger words! Bridie glanced at Peter as one after another came leaping out of the story.

"And mind you," Liz was saying, "I knew Faulkner by reputation every damn bit as well as the lassie that gave Bridie the warnin'. Even the cat, we used to say, was no' safe when he was around. An' when I saw her standin' there, the poor wee innocent, wi' her eyes blazin' blue murder at the very thought of him and the tears still wet on her face—"

The children were openmouthed, husband John was openmouthed, but Peter's face was white and stretched with fury.

"I could have killed him," Liz made her final flourish, "wi' less thought than I would have killed a fly!"

Peter said through his teeth, "I *will* kill him—the rotten bastard! I *will* kill him!"

"No, you'll not," Liz contradicted. "For the very reason that he's very likely off to the war now, same as you are, and well out of your reach. Besides, the lassie's none the worse for it—for which you can thank that spirit she showed—and it's all long over and done with now."

"Aye, man." Husband John spoke up for the first time. "And you're all the less likely to run into him,

224

seeing he's not the kind to risk getting his feet wet in the Andrew."

Peter's eyes widened in surprise. "How d'you know that word?" he asked. "Have you done time in the Navy?"

"Aye. In the last war. Torpedoman, I was. Same as yourself."

"Well, I'm damned!" With interest further dispelling his anger, Peter hitched his chair closer to that of Fat Liz's husband, and under cover of their continued conversation, Liz herself turned to whisper to Bridie:

"How did I do, hen?"

"You did fine, you cunning old vixen!" Bridie grinned again at her. "You did just what I wanted you to do."

Liz gave a slow, complacent wink. "Aye, so I guessed. Or you'd never have mentioned Faulkner's name in the first place. I'm not so green as I'm cabbage-lookin', am I?"

"You're certainly not! And thanks, Liz. Thanks for clearing it all up for me."

"Away with you! D'you think I was never a lassie myself, wi' all a lassie's fears and worries?" Fat Liz rose, queenly and dignified as ever. "But he has the truth of it now. He knows that none of it was your fault, and so it's time—eh?—to make some tea for everybody."

"No, let me!" Bridie also rose, and then biting her lip on laughter, she added, "Please, Your Majesty."

"What's that?" Liz was puzzled for a moment. Then

225

she laughed her rich, chortling laugh, and said, "So you're back to that nonsense you talked in the hospital, are you? Well, I'll say this for you. You're persistent!"

They moved together into the kitchen, and once there Liz went on, "And I'll tell you somethin' else hen. I meant it when I said you have a good lad there. So just you go out now and enjoy your courtin' days wi' him. Because that's what God made lads and lassies for, and those days, hen, are sweet ones. Take it from me. They're the sweetest you'll ever have."

They were days of sunshine too, the first of the spring and summer that everyone was later to remember as having been unusually warm that year. Days for the open air, all of them.

Each morning they went out together from the city, Bridie mounted on William's bicycle, Peter on a rusty machine rescued from his father's garden shed. They made long, exploratory runs along country lanes where the verges were splashed with the bright yellow of celandines, and the low beech hedges were vivid with new green. Peter reverted to a boyhood passion for fishing, taught Bridie how to use one of his rods, and they left their bicycles to walk for miles up the narrow trout streams—the peat burns—of the Pentland Hills, with small fronds of green bracken uncurling at their feet, and here and there a wild cherry tree standing, white as a bride, in its fragile drift of blossom.

"You could find better things to fish for than these

tiddlers," Uncle George said sourly when they brought home a bag of the small, speckled burn trout. Uncle George was still resenting Bridie's demand for time off, but the little trout had pink, firm flesh that made sweet eating, and he tackled them with gusto all the same.

Bridie took Peter to visit the village of her childhood, and they raced barefoot along the sandy shore of the Firth of Forth, gathered whelks and buckies, and mussels, boiled them in a tin can over a fire of driftwood, and picked the contents of the shells out with a pin.

"Just like the Others and I used to do," Bridie contentedly remembered.

They went even farther afield for their fishing, and the trout they brought back for Peter's mother to cook were of more respectable size than Uncle George's tiddlers.

"You're like a couple of kids playing," she told them indulgently, and they did not contradict her or tell her what they both instinctively felt—that to walk, to run, to cycle, to climb, to breathe in as much as they could of sun and wind, to see and feel the aliveness of blossom and leaf and earth and water, was a way of asserting their own aliveness, and of defying the war to take it from them. Or from each other.

In the Braid Park where they wandered each evening, this, they knew, was what they were defying. But in the Braid Park, too, their defiance took a form that was very different from the energetic one of the

227

childish daytime pursuits. They spoke low and, when they sat with the shimmer of the pond before them, were content often with silence.

In the dusk of the woodland, walking with the pale stars of the primroses at their feet, they were acutely aware of their physical nearness to one another; and so there they went slowly, savoring each moment that brought a look, a touch of the hand. They paused sometimes to kiss, with neither of them knowing how the moment of pause had arrived. And it was after one such moment, one such kiss, that Peter said:

"I love you, Bridie. I think I always have loved you."

Bridie said, "I love you, Peter. And I know I always will."

24

Their conversations in the Braid Park became scattered with confessions to one another, some of these foolish ones, and some serious.

"It was your hair that first attracted me to you," Peter said. "I used to sit in that class at the Bellwood and watch it shining so soft and fair under the light and wonder what it would feel like to stroke it."

"Is that why you went hunting for me through all those flower shops—just to stroke my hair?"

Peter laughed. "No, stupid! It was something else about you. You were always so intent on what you were doing, so determined. And yet—maybe it's that wide-eyed look you have—you always seemed so vulnerable too. I used to want to cuddle you and tell you I wouldn't let anybody hurt you."

"I used to look at you," she confessed, "when you

weren't looking at me. I nearly wrote in my exercise book once, *Peter McKinley's dark, Peter McKinley's handsome.*" She leaned towards him, her movement arousing the faint scent of the primroses in the grass beneath them. "When did you first know you loved me?"

"When I was running away from you, down the Assembly steps. But—" Peter paused for a moment. "There are nights at sea, you know, when you're sailing along in a dead calm, blackout and radio silence imposed on the whole convoy, the sky an inky black with the stars very big and bright. Or perhaps there's a full moon. But either of these sort of nights is the most dangerous time for a convoy, because that's when a sub can get the ships in silhouette against the light in the sky. That's when the watch is supposed to be most alert. And yet—" He raised himself with his weight resting on one hand, so that he could look down into her face. "I thought I'd found the distraction I wanted when I went off to the Navy, but it's since then—and especially when I've been standing watch on one of those calm, bright nights—that I've imagined myself thousands of times running back up the Assembly steps just to tell you what I should have told you then."

"I thought I'd lost you forever," Bridie said.

"I thought I'd lost you—till you sent me that first part of 'The Cloths of Heaven.'"

He let himself gently down to her and kissed her. The heat of his body reached hers, and there was the same fire in her own. What would she do, she won-

230

dered, if he wanted more this time than a kiss? She was what men like Jack Taylor called "a nice girl." And there was a code that said "nice girls don't." Besides which, she'd vowed—hadn't she?—that she wouldn't make a mess of her life the way Bunty had done, that it *would* always be *her* life to be kept in *her* hands. But Peter wasn't her flash man. Peter was her love, her true, true love, and he was going off to sea again. Peter could be dead in a few days' time. . . .

"Hey, hey!" Peter's hands on her face found the overflowing tears. "You're crying!"

"It's you!" The words were out before Bridie could stop them. "I've seen the way your father and mother look at you. I know what they're feeling, and it's what I feel too. I'm so afraid for you!"

She struggled up, brushing away her tears, wishing with all her heart now that the words could also be brushed away. Peter sat up beside her and waited for a moment before he said:

"There's no point in that, you know—in your being afraid for me. That won't get either of us anywhere."

She turned to look at him, taken aback by the calmness of his tone. "But aren't you afraid for yourself?"

"Sometimes," he admitted. "When I hear the 'Action Stations' call. Everybody's afraid then, I think. But it can't last because you have a job to do; and if you're not quick about it you just increase whatever danger there is."

"And what about the rest of the time?"

Peter shrugged. "I think the way everyone else does. Somewhere there might be a bomb or a torpedo with my number on it, in which case, I'll get it. If there isn't, I won't. That's how simple it is—because you'd go stark, staring bonkers in a week, you know, if you didn't think like that."

"I wish—" Bridie faltered for a moment. "I didn't want to make it harder for you. I wish I'd kept my big mouth shut."

"Nonsense!" Peter teased. "It's a charming mouth."

"No." Bridie shook her head. "I talk too much."

"I like to hear you talk. Talk to me now." Peter settled himself comfortably back in the grass. "Tell me when you first knew you loved me."

"The day you came on leave. Here, beside the pond, when you said there'd never be enough time to spend with me. It's odd, you know." Bridie turned to look down at him, smiling now at her own sudden recollections. "I thought I'd been in love hundreds of times before then—well, a few times, anyway. Mostly with the Dutchmen who come to sell bulbs for Spring flowers to Uncle George. They're all marvelously good-looking men, you see, with flashing white teeth that show a lot because they talk so enthusiastically about the bulb fields of Holland. And all in perfect English, too! I used to get fearful crushes on them. And then there was a senior boy from Watson's school who was always very charming to me when he came in for flowers for his mother. I used to stand primping in front of the mirror when I expected to see him—"

"That's enough!" Peter seized her, wrestled her to the ground, and commanded, "You're sorry about all that now. Say you're sorry!"

"Won't! I won't!" She struggled against the hold that had her pinned, laughing and repeating her defiance. And Peter was more than strong enough to keep her there, and he was laughing as much as she was, but suddenly he was breaking away to sit with his head in his hands while he said shakily:

"Oh God, oh God, Bridie! You just don't know what you're doing to me, do you?"

Bridie lay in silence waiting for him to recover his composure, and trying hard, also, to recover her own. If only, she thought, if only Peter realized that she knew very well how hard it was for him to ask no more than kisses. And how hard it had become for her to offer no more! She opened her mouth on the temptation to speak and then closed it again.

Peter, she warned herself, had come home with the deliberate intention of courting her. Peter accepted the code that applied to "nice girls." And how could she make it harder for him now when the code laid down that courtship had to lead to marriage—or to nothing at all!

They came across a patch of wood violets one night in the Braid Park, and with a cry of pleasure, Bridie knelt beside them.

"My mother's favorite flower," she told Peter. "I remember—" *But no, she did not want to remember the child who'd been reaching out for violets and had fallen facedown instead into the pile of lambs' tails lying all bloody where the shepherd had chopped them off.*

Peter sat down beside her and said, "Every time

you say 'I remember' and stop the way you did just now, I have the feeling you're thinking about the time in your life that you don't want to remember, the time your father died. Am I right?"

"Yes." She spoke quietly, her face turned away from him. "My mother was grieving so. I went to pick violets to try and make her happy again, and it all ended like one of the nightmares I used to have after he died."

Peter put a hand over hers. His was warm, comforting. He let it lie there for a moment before he asked, "But it's better for you now, isn't it?"

"Yes. I think I've learned to live with it. There's more . . . more . . ." She searched for the right word and found it in a sudden memory of the portrait in the locket. "There's more tenderness now than pain."

Peter's grip on her hand tightened. "I'm glad."

They sat in silence, the scent of the violets all around them. Peter said eventually, "I remember, too, Bridie. I remember the day you first spoke to me about it, here in the Braid. You told me then that you'd always be haunted by the sense of pursuing Time it had given you. And I wondered—" With the last of his words left hanging in the air, he turned to look intently at her; and quietly, Bridie finished the sentence for him:

"—if that's still true for me?" He nodded; and quietly again she said, "Yes, it's still true. And it's still the thing that tells me I *must* write."

"I was afraid of that," Peter told her. "You're too intense, Bridie. Far too intense. And it's not good for you."

"But it's the only way I can be!" Bridie sat back,

biting her lip in dismay. It wasn't possible, was it, that he was going to tell her she should give up writing? Rebellion flared in her, and with the sound of it in her voice, she added, "You can't make me any different, either. Nobody can."

Peter turned a puzzled look on her. "Who spoke of making you different?"

"Nobody—yet! But if you tried to forbid—"

"Forbid!" Peter caught her up on the word, surprise in his voice. "You do have to be handled with tongs, don't you! I've had my share of using that word, thank you, and I don't need to be told again that it won't work with you."

"So what *are* you trying to say?"

"Something that should be obvious even to you, you ninny. That you need someone to look after you."

"I'm not a baby," she objected. "I'm almost eighteen."

Peter brushed her words aside and asked, "Bridie, d'you remember that night beside the Scott Monument?"

"Of course." She nodded, smiling at the memory.

"Well, suppose now—" Peter hesitated. "Just suppose I was wrong to encourage you that night. Suppose you never do make it as a writer. What then?"

"You weren't wrong. I'll make it. I *know* I will."

"All right. Suppose then, that you make it in a small way, but never find fame and fortune?"

"Then I'll never get swellheaded, will I?" Bridie laughed as she spoke, but when Peter did not respond to her laugh, she leaned towards him and asked coax-

235

ingly, "Peter, do *you* remember the first day we talked, and how you told me that trying to catch even one of my ideas was like trying to catch a dragonfly?"

"I remember."

"Yes. And I remember boasting that someday I'd make the right net of words to capture all those big, bright ideas of mine. But I've thought since then, Peter. I've thought that it would take a really great writer to succeed in that. And I'm not great! But I do at least know where I'm going now in my writing, and so I can at least take some hold on those ideas. In fact—" She smiled again, at the thought shaping in her mind. "There's your answer, my lad! To hell with fame and fortune so long as I can write, even in a small way, of big things."

"Bridie—" Peter spoke her name with an odd, broken note in his voice. She waited for him to go on, but instead of that he rose, then reached out a hand to pull her up beside him. She stood looking up at his face hovering pale over her in the dusk. He spoke again, and said:

"Will you marry me?"

His voice was shaky, and very quiet. She had thought it would be so easy to say "Yes," but her voice, when she made to answer, had gone altogether. Peter tried again.

"I love you. I need you. I know you love me. And God knows you need me to look after you. Will you marry me?"

"Yes." The word was out at last, and it was only a whisper. But it was enough.

25

Four A.M. and the only train expected in at the Waverley Station was the London one, the only lights burning were the dim blue lamps that stretched the gray concrete length of platform 7. Bridie wondered if there could be a deader place or a drearier time. Yet outside, the gardens lining the south side of Princes Street would be waking to the dawn of a summer day—early June, with the grass a fresh, bright green, and all the roses in bloom.

For a moment or two she was tempted to walk back up the slope of the Carriage Drive. The London train was late—three hours late, according to the message chalked on the board at the gate of the platform, and waiting beside the gardens would be more bearable than three hours spent in this gloomy cave of a place.

But supposing the message was wrong? Supposing that some, at least, of the chaos among trains from the south had been sorted out? That could mean missing the arrival of the London, missing her first glimpse of Peter stepping off it. And that, after all her strenuous efforts to get there on time, was surely something she couldn't risk now.

A clatter and a banging as a porter came along noisily wheeling a trolley loaded with milk churns. A louder clattering as the churns were off-loaded to the edge of the platform; then the trolley was pushed back against the platform's boundary rail, and at last there was somewhere to sit. As Bridie perched herself on the trolley, two of the other figures scattered along the platform's dim length began working their way towards this solitary chance of a seat. She watched their approach, wondering vaguely if their feet were aching as badly as her own.

Three miles! It had been a long walk from Comiston. A frightening one, too, with nobody except herself in the rain and dark and wind of the predawn streets, no buses or trams running, not a taxi in sight. And worst of all had been that moment, that terrible moment when she had been passing the police box at Tollcross and the air-raid siren mounted on top of the box had blasted off right in her ear, and just as that happened the wind had blown her umbrella inside out and an air-raid warden had shouted and blown his whistle at her, and instead of dying of fright as she had thought she would then, she had just dropped her umbrella and ran and ran and *ran*!

The two figures converging on her were those of a woman and a girl. The woman, she thought, was built like Fat Liz, but it was only in build that any resemblance existed. This woman had soft, spreading features around a fleshy, self-satisfied mouth. Her clothes were typical of middle-aged, middle-class Edinburgh; and her voice, the genteel, overrefined "Thenk yoh!" of it as Bridie moved to make room for her, was also typical Edinburgh middle-class.

The girl hovered for a moment before she allowed herself to sit beside the genteel lady; but the girl, Bridie noted, was a tinker. All the signs of it were there on her: the sharp features, the sun-browned skin, the bare legs below a dress that was quite obviously someone's cast-off, the shabby coat that might once have fitted a short, fat man, and that now hung loosely from her own slim shoulders. And yet, it was equally obvious, too, that this tinker had taken *some* pains with her appearance. Her face and her bare legs were at least clean, and although she hadn't been very successful in combing her dark hair, she had tied a ribbon bow in it.

Bridie's eyes lingered on the ribbon. The tinker girl, she judged, was about the same age as herself. And yet the ribbon was pink, a pale pink, the color a child might be given to wear. But perhaps that was the only ribbon the tinker girl had been able to get hold of. Or perhaps, if it was her young man she was going to meet off the train and if pale pink was his favorite color, she didn't mind how unsuitable it looked on an eighteen-year-old. The large lady spoke, her gaze on Bridie's left hand.

"Aih see you're engaged."

Bridie found herself blushing as she always did when someone noticed the ring Mr. Finkelstein had helped Peter and herself to choose on the final day of his leave in March. Over two months ago, and she still hadn't got used to seeing it there on her finger! With a nod and a murmur of agreement to the large lady, she let her mind drift back to that day at the end of March when they had sat in Mr. Finkelstein's back shop with the tray of rings spread out in front of them, and Mr. Finkelstein had insisted on giving them their choice at trade price. Then he had poured glasses of sherry, so that they could all drink a toast together—but there was that damned woman talking again, the genteel tones forcing themselves insistently on her hearing! "Your feeawnsay." Something about "your feeawnsay." And what the devil was that? Rapidly Bridie made the leap in understanding to "fiancé" as the large lady repeated:

"Aind is your feeawnsay in the Ermy?"

"Ermy"—that was "Army," of course. Bridie fought down a hysterical impulse to parody the strangled vowels, and said gravely:

"No. The Navy." And still alive, thank God, even although his ship had gone down and it was Survivor's Leave that was bringing him home!

"May husband," said the large lady, "is Ermy." Complacently she crossed her legs, rested her clasped hands on her knees, and with even greater complacency allowed the gesture to show the third finger of her left hand loaded with wedding ring, eternity ring,

240

and an engagement ring set with a solitaire diamond so large that it flashed even under the dim blue of the station's wartime lighting. In a tone that matched her gesture with the rings, she added, "He's an awfficer, of course. On the Steff."

On the Staff! And how very nice, Bridie thought, to have been married all these past two months to someone safely tucked away in an office somewhere in England, while all Mr. Finkelstein's predictions about the war in Europe at last came true: Denmark first, then Norway, then Belgium, Holland, and France, all going down under Hitler's latest *Blitzkrieg*! How very nice for the large lady, too, not having had to pace the floor every night while the British troops were being driven back out of Norway and one British ship after another was being blown to hell, not having had to make bargains with God that she would do anything He wanted, anything at all, if only He would arrange it that Peter's ship hadn't been one of those that had gone down there!

The fleshy, self-satisfied mouth was still talking. Bridie moved till her shoulder was hunched towards it. The woman, she realized, was one of those people who simply had to talk, simply had to have *someone* to impress. And she herself had become the victim, of course, because the woman was also the kind who wouldn't condescend even to notice the tinker girl.

The hunched shoulder did its work. Large lady got up after a few minutes and sauntered off in search of some other victim. Bridie checked the station clock and saw that the time was still only five-thirty. The

241

tinker girl, she noticed, had begun to throw glances at her, but however much the tinker might want to have a conversation with someone her own age, she would still be far too wary to be the one to start it. Bridie tried a smile towards her, and then said casually:

"You waiting for your fella?"

The tinker girl muttered an assent; then shyly she asked, "You waitin' for yours?"

Bridie nodded. "He's in the Navy. But his ship went down at Dunkirk, and he's coming home on Survivor's Leave."

The tinker said, "My fella's Army. Been in France for months. He was one o' them that fought right through, till the Jerries drove them back to Dunkirk."

"Mine's been on Western Approaches since the start of the war," Bridie offered. "On convoy duty. Till they had to use all the ships they could get, of course, to rescue the chaps off the beaches at Dunkirk. He phoned me at my work yesterday to tell me he was coming home."

"Mine sent a telegram to the Post Office near where my folk are now, an' the Postmaster had to deliver it."

Although he wouldn't have liked that, Bridie thought; a respectable Postmaster being forced to cycle out with a telegram vaguely addressed to some tinker encampment in his area!

"Did you hear on the radio what it's been like in France?" she asked.

"Aye." The tinker girl nodded, and on a long,

sighing intake of breath she added, "Terrible, eh?"

They sat in silence for several moments, the way people always did now when they thought of France and the past six weeks when its roads had been a panic mass of refugees, dive-bombed and machine-gunned as they fled the conquering advance of the German armored columns. Six weeks! It must have seemed a long time to them, but it was still hard to believe that it had taken the Germans *only* six weeks to enter Paris in triumph and drive the British soldiers back and back till they were seemingly trapped in that small area around Dunkirk.

"Your fella," the tinker girl said, "did a good job o' gettin' our chaps out o' that mess. All them Navy fellas did."

"I know. And so did the men with the little boats. Don't forget them." Don't forget the English civvies with their volunteer armada of small pleasure craft stubbornly plying back and forth between England and France, sailing in time and time again under the bombs and the machine-gunning to pick up men who would otherwise have died in the hot sun and sand of those French beaches—as poor Hughie had died, Hughie of the greasy curls and cheerful grin, Hughie the good-hearted keelie who had fought his last rammy at Dunkirk! Impulsively, Bridie turned to tell the tinker girl:

"They were brave, those civvy volunteers! I had a friend died at Dunkirk. But there would have been such an awful lot more dead if it hadn't been for them."

"Aye." The tinker nodded a solemn agreement. "An'

a lot more like me, that might've been made widows."

Involuntarily Bridie glanced at the girl's left hand that was bare of rings of any kind. The girl's eyes followed the look, and when she spoke again, it was with a smile beginning to light her face.

"My fella and me," she explained, "are as good as married. We're handfasted."

Bridie, too, began to smile. "Handfasted"—it was a word she hadn't heard since she was a child; a country word, a marvelous old country word! And of course, the girl was right! Any one of the various betrothal ceremonies that country people called "handfasting" *was* as good as a marriage—in their eyes, at least. And most certainly that would also be the case in a tinker encampment. The girl was smiling even more widely now, pleased with the effect of her declaration; and with a ring of pride in her voice, she added:

"I jumped through the fire wi' him."

Once, and only once, had Bridie seen the ritual of jumping through the fire—in the tinker encampment that had appeared annually beside her own village; and she had been no more than ten years old at the time. But even so, she had known, it was a scene that would remain vivid with her for the rest of her life: the old women building up the fire at the center of the ring of round, black tents, the brown-faced children running and tumbling with excitement, the group of men with lean dogs alert at their feet and dark eyes gleaming in anticipation above their mugs of beer, the younger women tying flowers into the hair of the girl who was to jump, while her young man stood apprehensively watching the fire being torched into life; and then finally, the young man and woman reaching hands to one another, holding still for a long moment and looking hard into one another's eyes before they ran, still hand in hand, towards the fire and jumped—jumped for their lives and for each other, through the flames!

Bridie looked enviously at the tinker. This one would come to know pain, of course, the way that other, older one had done. But still . . .

"You were lucky," she said, "to have had the chance."

"One night," the girl said. "One night before he was off to the war. That was all we had. But look!" She drew aside the flaps of her too-big coat to show a form swollen with pregnancy, and proudly added, "But he'll have a bairn to come home to now, as well as me!"

"My mum doesn't want me to get married this leave," Bridie confessed. "She says I'm too young. But I'm going to, all the same." *Hold on to love. Oh, Bridie girl, hold on to love!*

"Good for you!" the tinker girl told her. "Because there's no' much time left for us young 'uns, is there?"

245

26

How much time was there left for "young 'uns" like herself and the tinker girl?

It would not be long now before the Germans launched an attempt at invading Britain. Everyone was agreed on that. And everyone knew that Britain would have to stand alone when it did happen. Yet nobody was talking about giving up. Nobody was even thinking about that—except selfish idiots like the large lady, perhaps, or the bully boys who were creepy Henry's friends. And what did their kind matter when there was such a strong will to resist among so many others?

We shall fight on the beaches, we shall fight on the landing grounds, we shall fight in the fields and in the streets, we shall fight in the hills; we shall never surrender. . . .

The words of the great speech that had come out of Parliament, the speech of the new Prime Minister, Churchill, sounded their drumroll again in Bridie's mind. Yet still her question persisted. How much time was left before they had to face up to all that?

Even fragments of time were precious now! Her eyes went back and back again to the station clock. Six A.M., and platform 7 was becoming busier. The figures waiting for the train were growing in number. A boy with a bag of newspapers was moving among them. Beyond the railing that separated the platform from the station concourse, the woman at the flower stand was unpacking the roses she had brought down from Market Street. And outside the station altogether, Bridie thought, the June sunshine would be bright now on the grass and the massed roses in Princes Street Gardens, on the Castle, too, on the High Street, on all of the Old Town that she and Peter had loved so well.

The tinker girl had risen to wander down to one end of the platform. Bridie got to her feet and began walking slowly in the opposite direction. There was a letter from Peter in her handbag, the last one he had managed to send before Dunkirk. She took it out and hungrily re-read the salutation at the head of the page. *My dear and only love.* He had been quoting there, of course, but how often had she quoted to him when she had found her own words inadequate to express her feelings?

Soberly, as she tucked the letter back into her handbag, she told herself, "It was true what I said to him.

I'll never be great." Never be one of the few whose light leapt far beyond that of all the little flames around them! The idea of herself as a small flame stubbornly burning brought a smile to her face.

The dragonfly years, she thought, all those past years of loosing her flight of big and bright ideas into the air and then trying to capture them all again on one small sheet of paper each time she sat down to write; those years hadn't really been wasted! They had been practice, instead, for shaping all the tales still moving in her mind, for making perfect the patterns of lovely words still stored there. And her flame now would at least be a clear one!

Bridie glanced yet again at the station clock. Six-thirty. Mum would be getting Granda's breakfast now. Granda was too old these days to be at Market Street with Uncle George sharp on the dot of six when all the flower wholesalers opened for the day. In half an hour Mum would call her, find she wasn't there but gone to meet the train, and then the fuss about her being too young to get married would start all over again. But she would talk Mum round. Peter's parents approved, after all, which meant they would help to persuade her. And even the fact that they weren't getting married in church might help, because church weddings were costly, and apart from the housekeeping money Granda gave her, Mum still didn't have two pennies to rub together.

Bridie turned and strolled in the opposite direction. The tinker girl had jumped through the fire. She herself would be married in a Registry Office. Simple ceremonies, both of them. And so there wasn't really that much difference between them—except, of course, that jumping through the fire had been a dramatic gesture. And the tinker girl had at least worn flowers twined in her hair— The train had been signaled! There was a bright blob of green showing on the signal away down at the far end of the platform!

Bridie hung back against the railing, afraid she might miss Peter in the crowd of people beginning to press forward to the platform's edge. A plume of smoke, a rumbling noise growing louder and louder, a gleam of brass fittings as the front of the engine appeared, voices all around, talking, laughing, shouting, a forest of hands beginning to wave from the people on the platform, from the windows of the train itself—and there it was pulling in, a long slow line of coaches with every door swinging open as it slid to a long, slow halt beside the platform.

A hand clutched Bridie's arm. "There he is! There! There!" It was the tinker girl, holding on to her and pointing with the other hand to the soldiers tumbling out of one coach.

The tinker made a dash towards the soldiers. Bridie found her view temporarily obscured by the reappearance of the large lady making expansive gestures as she ordered a porter to follow her with his lugguage trolley. The platform had become a seethe of Servicemen—soldiers mostly, swinging kitbags around, greeting civilians, shouting back and forth to one another.

Bridie's gaze skimmed frantically over the khaki-colored mass, saw a flash of white, another flash—on navy blue, this time—and then the khaki scrum split apart and there was a solid phalanx of sailors in their navy blue and white bearing down on her, and Peter was leading it, calling, waving to her, breaking into a run, just as he had that day in Comiston.

Somehow, when they got out through the gate of the platform, the sailors were still with them. Some of them were Peter's shipmates. All of them were on Survivor's Leave. That much she had learned in the struggle to get clear of the crowd on the platform. Other girls had been met and swept along with them, some older women too, and now they were all standing breathless and smiling at the foot of the Carriage Drive while Peter said commandingly:

"Wait here! Right? All of you."

The girls glanced in surprise at one another, then at Bridie, and she did not know where to look. But the sailors, as Peter turned away from the group, all grinned at one another; and a second later, she understood the reason for the grins. Peter had dashed over to the flower seller's stand, swept up an armful of roses, and thrown down some money, and now he was dashing back to her.

Nor was that all. Once Peter had arrived back at the group and thrust the flowers into her arms, he flashed a glance around the rest of the sailors, and asked:

"Right, mateys?"

There was an answering chorus of "Aye, aye, Jack!" The sailors moved forward on their own shout and pushed a way into the press of people and traffic in the Carriage Drive, loudly calling as they went, "Gangway for the bride! Gangway for the bride!"

Heads turned towards them. People smiled, and good-naturedly stepped out of their way. A taxi-driver grinned from behind his glass windscreen, and pulled his vehicle over to one side of the Carriage Drive. The sailors formed a double line along the path they had cleared. Peter offered Bridie his arm.

At the far end of the Carriage Drive where the roses were blooming in Princes Street Gardens, Bridie could see an arch of sky showing the mixture of sunshine and cloud that was Edinburgh's usual summer weather. Peter was smiling at her. The blue of his eyes was very bright. She shifted her impromptu bouquet to her right arm, and slipped her left hand around the arm Peter had offered.

"I love you," he said.

"I love you," Bridie answered, and began walking with him through their guard of honor, out of the station's wartime dimness and into the uncertain promise of the day ahead.